By Kalynn Bayron

FOR YOUNGER READERS
The Vanquishers

FOR OLDER READERS
Cinderella Is Dead
·
This Poison Heart
This Wicked Fate
·
You're Not Supposed to Die Tonight

YOU'RE NOT SUPPOSED TO DIE TONIGHT

KALYNN BAYRON

BLOOMSBURY

NEW YORK   LONDON   OXFORD   NEW DELHI   SYDNEY

BLOOMSBURY YA
Bloomsbury Publishing Inc., part of Bloomsbury Publishing Plc
1385 Broadway, New York, NY 10018

BLOOMSBURY and the Diana logo are trademarks of Bloomsbury Publishing Plc

First published in the United States of America in June 2023 by Bloomsbury YA

Bloomsbury books may be purchased for business or promotional use. For information
on bulk purchases please contact Macmillan Corporate and Premium Sales Department at
specialmarkets@macmillan.com

This is a work of fiction. Names, characters, businesses, places, events, locales, and incidents are either
the products of the author's imagination or used in a fictitious manner. Any resemblance to actual
persons, living or dead, or actual events is purely coincidental.

Library of Congress Cataloging-in-Publication Data
Names: Bayron, Kalynn, author.
Title: You're not supposed to die tonight / by Kalynn Bayron.
Other titles: You are not supposed to die tonight
Description: New York : Bloomsbury, 2023.
Summary: Seventeen-year-old Charity's role of playing the "final girl" at Camp Mirror Lake,
where guests pay to be scared, becomes all too real when her coworkers begin disappearing, and
if she and her girlfriend, Bezi, want to survive, they will need to figure out what the killer is after.
Identifiers: LCCN 2022048706
ISBN 978-1-5476-1154-6 (hardcover) • ISBN 978-1-5476-1155-3 (e-book)
Subjects: CYAC: Supernatural—Fiction. | Lesbians—Fiction. | Horror stories. |
LCGFT: Horror fiction. | Novels.
Classification: LCC PZ7.1.B386 Yo 2023 | DDC [Fic]—dc23
LC record available at https://lccn.loc.gov/2022048706

Book design by John Candell
Typeset by Westchester Publishing Services
Printed and bound in the U.S.A.
2 4 6 8 10 9 7 5 3 1

To find out more about our authors and books visit www.bloomsbury.com
and sign up for our newsletters.

For Final Girls everywhere

CHAPTER 1

My hands are smeared with blood. Dirt sticks under my nails. My jeans are ripped at the knee, and my T-shirt is stained because I had to claw my way out from my hiding spot under the supply cabin. He is too close, and I can't risk staying here.

Above me, the moon is just a sliver of silver hanging in the sky, but I'm thankful. I lost my flashlight, and the moon is now the only thing lighting the path in front of me as I push toward the main lodge.

The boathouse comes into view. I suck in a chest full of chilly nighttime air and let out a bloodcurdling scream. It carries in the clear, quiet dark. Three people burst from the boathouse. They're tripping all over one another, and the woman is screaming her face off. The two dudes with her look pretty shaken up.

"Help me!" I scream. I limp toward them, panting, clutching my side. "Please help me!"

The woman runs up to me and grabs me by the shoulders, digging her nails into my skin.

"I gotta get out of here!" she shrieks. "I didn't know it was going to be like this! I can't do this."

She has a raised welt on the side of her face, and her bottom lip is split open.

"It's just the three of you left?" I ask as I try to catch my breath.

"Yeah," says one of the other guys. His gaze darts from me to the lake, which is flat calm and looks like a giant black mirror reflecting the silvery sliver of moon in the sky.

Somewhere behind me, a branch snaps, like something heavy is crushing it underfoot. My heart slams in my chest. The woman leans over and puts her hands on her knees. She doesn't appear to have heard the sound. Her back is to the woods when suddenly, he's there. His dark-blue coveralls are smudged with dirt, making him almost impossible to see against the backdrop of towering pines. His six-foot-eight frame looms in the shadows like a ghost. His mask is horrifying in the dark. It's a dingy white color, smeared with red and mud. There's a crack running up the right side. His massive hand grips the handle of a machete, its blade slick with blood.

He stalks forward, and the woman doesn't even see him until it's too late. He grabs her from behind, lifting her up off the ground. He disappears with her kicking and screaming into the Mason Lodge, a smaller cabin we mostly use for storage. I don't move. I can't.

One of the guys makes a break for it and bolts toward the camp entrance. The other guy just stands there as a thin film of sweat blankets his forehead. I grab his arm, and he snaps out of whatever terror-induced trance he's in and starts hollering as loud as he can.

"Come on!" I yell.

The dirt road that leads to the camp's main entrance seems too long, and the screams of the terrified woman echo all around us as we race down it. The timbers of the giant sign that flank the entry gate materialize out of the dark. The other man is already there.

"Brandon!" he screams. "Get your ass over here! We gotta go!"

"What about Leslie?" Brandon asks. "We can't just leave her!"

"Leave her ass here!" the other man screams.

A body lies motionless on the ground in the main parking lot. Tasha. My friend, my coworker for the past summer, is lying on her stomach. The glinting handle of a large knife protrudes from her back. A dark stain seeps across her yellow uniform shirt.

Brandon sees her and staggers forward, clawing at the iron gate, which is padlocked shut.

I stagger to the gate and grab the metal bars. I push on them and scream as loud as I can.

"Help us! Please! Somebody help us!"

On the other side of the locked gate, the machete-wielding, masked figure appears.

"No!" I scream. "Leave us alone! What do you want?"

The two dudes cling to each other. Tears trail down Brandon's face.

The masked man stalks forward as I grip the metal entrance gate. I don't move, even though my gut is telling me to run. He walks up and grabs the front of my shirt through the bars. I struggle in his grip, clawing at him, kicking against the bars.

He glares down at me with eyes black as coal. I reach into the waistband of my jeans and pull out a butcher knife. I plunge it into the killer's chest, and blood flows from the wound. He lets go of my shirt and staggers back. As he cries out, he drops his machete, falls flat on his back, and goes completely limp.

It's over.

I slowly turn around and look the last two dudes directly in the eye.

I smile.

It's never easy at the end. I'm trying so hard to hold in my laughter, I can't help but chuckle a little as I make the announcement.

"I am the final girl," I say. The floodlights click on, washing the entrance in a bright white light. "And you two have survived a night at Camp Mirror Lake. You win!"

The men stare slack-jawed at me as people descend on the

scene. The other Camp Mirror Lake staff crowd around us, and the other guests who'd been eliminated earlier in the night reappear. Tasha resurrects herself and scrambles to her feet, the knife rig still attached to her body. I wipe my mouth with the back of my hand, and the sickly sweet corn syrup sticks to my lips. Someone cues the music; the Halloween theme song blasts through the camp.

Leslie, the chick who got snatched up by the Mason Lodge, pushes her way through the crowd, marches up to Brandon, and slaps him so hard that spit flies out of his mouth. The entire crowd goes silent.

"You left me!" she screams. "You ran away!"

Kyle, the masked killer who is actually a classmate of mine at Groton High School, reemerges sans mask holding a T-shirt that says, I SURVIVED THE NIGHT AT CAMP MIRROR LAKE. It's the prize for "winning" the game, but when he hands it to Brandon, Leslie snatches it away and throws it on the ground, stomping on it until it's covered in mud. She breaks up with Brandon on the spot with the entire staff looking on.

Kyle leans in close to me, and I have to crane my neck to look up at him.

"Charity, we knocked this one out of the park."

I eye the dark-red stain on his chest. "I didn't hurt you, did I? I saw you wince. I'm so sorry."

He shakes his head and hands me back my retractable butcher knife. "It didn't collapse into the handle all the way. Thought you stabbed me for real for a minute." He chuckles.

"I'm good. I hope you never actually get mad at me, though."
He rubs his chest and grins.

This is one of the top three nights of the season, hands
down. I'm so proud of us. I feel bad for Brandon and his now-
ex-girlfriend, but they knew what they signed up for. What
matters in this moment is that the game was a raging success,
and now I'm ready to shower, knock out in my cabin, and do it
all over again the following night.

• • •

After two summers—the first as fake-blood cleanup staff and
the second as Staff Victim #3—I finally got promoted to the
most coveted position in the entire park—Final Girl. *The* final
girl to be exact.

Camp Mirror Lake is a full-contact terror-simulation experience. We run the whole thing on the location used during the
filming of the 1983 cult classic *The Curse of Camp Mirror Lake*.
As far as slasher films go, it's somewhere between *Friday the
13th* and *Scream*. A classic, but a little cheesy if I'm being honest. It chronicled the bloody rampage of inhuman serial killer
Scott Addison as he slashed his way through an eighties summer camp full of campers and their inept teenage counselors.
Now we re-create the events of the movie for groups of paid
guests. They come to be scared, but they almost always under-
estimate what's about to happen to them.

The Camp Mirror Lake experience requires all guests to
sign a thirty-three-page waiver. Nobody ever reads the whole

thing, but it explicitly states that staff members are allowed to push, shove, and restrain the guests. We're cleared to terrify each and every person who signs on the dotted line. It's always funny to me to see people upset at the end of the night. You signed a waiver that said a man in a mask can stalk you through the woods, but all of a sudden it's too real? But it never fails, and that's why Camp Mirror Lake has the reputation it does. We don't have a marketing budget. We don't have commercials or billboards—we have word of mouth and that's it. We have to dial the fear up to ten so the guests can run home and tell all their friends how scared they were. That's what keeps people, with what I'm convinced is some kind of masochistic streak, coming up here night after night.

As our season approaches its end, I'm left planning for the final Camp Mirror Lake experience—the biggest night of our season. We put everything into it, and this year is going to be the best send-off in Camp Mirror Lake history. I can feel it in my bones. We have brand-new squibs, a better recipe for more realistic-looking fake blood, and I'm way too excited to see Kyle use the newly renovated trapdoor in the main lodge to pop up on unsuspecting guests who always think it's a good idea to hide in the kitchen. Only three more days until the big show, and I'm so hyped I can hardly stand it.

Our checkout policy states that all guests must exit the camp as soon as the game officially ends, and that means seeing people off at nearly one in the morning. After I check everyone out, including Brandon and his now-ex-girlfriend,

Leslie, I do my final walk through of the main office and the western lodge; then I retreat to Lakeview Cabin #1, the place I call home for most of the summer.

Every time a game ends, its conclusion brings me one step closer to having to go home. I'd rather be out in these woods being chased by a fake serial killer than head home to Groton where my mom and her boyfriend, Rob, can pretend I don't exist. We live in Cedra Court, a motel that had been converted into apartments sometime in the late nineties. I think that might have been the worst idea anyone has ever had. It never really feels like home, just a place to stay.

In my mom's eyes, Rob can do no wrong even though Rob, at his big age, can't hold a job, and there's a permanent outline of his body on the couch because he sits in the same spot every single day. He drinks too much and spends my mom's money like she's not working two jobs just to stay afloat, but somehow *I'm* still the biggest problem he has. The best thing he's ever done for me is hand me the job listing for Camp Mirror Lake.

I shake myself, trying to somehow reverse the rot those memories have caused. I take out my earpiece to clean it off. Fake blood is caked around the little cord that connects the earpiece to the battery pack that clips on to the waist of my jeans. I pineapple my hair, tuck it under a plastic cap, grab my shower kit and a flashlight, and slip on my shower shoes. The cabins don't have private showers, so I have to make my way to the community stalls.

I can feel the fake blood sucking the moisture right out of

my skin. When I leave it on too long, it makes me break out, so I try to get it off before I go to sleep. I'm so tired I can barely keep my eyes open, but just because I'm in the middle of the woods in upstate New York, playing the final girl in a horror simulation, doesn't mean I should abandon my skin-care routine.

Pulling the door closed behind me, I step out onto the porch. The light outside my door is strong and steady. I stuck a hundred-watt bulb in the socket, and now it shines like a miniature sun and hums so loud, I low-key feel like it might explode at any moment. The air is wet and warm—summertime air—and that guarantees I'll have to keep my hair curly for the duration of the season because pressing it would be pointless. But there's always a little bit of a breeze coming off the lake, and that makes the heat bearable most of the time. It's so quiet after the guests have gone and the rest of the staff turn in for the night. There's an air of calm that stands in stark contrast to the frenzied chaos that had taken place only a little while before.

I jog down the steps, and they creak loudly. I hang a left and circle around the back of my cabin. The dirt path that leads to the showers is unlit. It's on this path that Victim #2 meets their grisly fate during our terror simulation. There are little bits of fake guts and dark patches of fake blood still on the ground. I'll have to lay down a fresh coat of dirt before the next group of guests arrives, but for now, I just step around it, trying not to get it on my shower shoes.

The moon isn't much help on the path due to the thick tree cover, so I flip on my flashlight and shine it in the direction of the showers. A branch breaks to my left, and I spin around. My heart stutters. Something small and furry creeps along the ground, eyes glinting in the glare of my flashlight. A raccoon. I push out a chest full of air and snap my fingers in its direction.

"Go on," I say. "Get out of here."

The raccoon looks at me like *I'm* the one in the wrong, then waddles off into the dark.

I try to get my heart to settle back into some kind of normal rhythm as I climb the steps to the community showers. I grab my key, but as I go to put it in the lock, I find that the main door is already unlocked and sitting slightly ajar. I shine my light through the cracked door.

"Do not play with me," I say aloud. I reach into my shower kit, pull out a can of Mace, and flip off the safety. "I will Mace you and I won't feel bad about it."

Silence.

The hair on the back of my neck stands straight up. My flashlight falters, blinking on and off twice.

"Don't you dare," I say, knocking it against the doorframe until the beam of light is continuous and steady.

Now, in this situation, horror films tell us that the final girl might go ahead and enter the community showers, disrobe, and then barely escape a masked killer as she slips around butt naked in the bathroom. However, I only play a final girl at

Camp Mirror Lake; I don't actually want to be one. I turn my Black ass right around and book it back to my cabin, where I close and lock the door. For now, my face full of fake blood is going to stay just the way it is.

My phone buzzes on the nightstand.

KYLE: Jordan and Heather were MIA earlier so I had to run the trapdoors myself. Annoying.

ME: Where'd they go?

KYLE: No idea. But if they don't come back it's just gonna be me, you, Tasha, Porter, and Javier. We'll have to shut everything down ourselves.

I roll my eyes. People either take this job way too seriously or not seriously enough. Me and Kyle have been the only consistent staff members since I started here. Everyone else from my first summer quit. Last season, my friend Tasha and a mutual friend of ours named Porter joined the crew, but some people we bring on are way too aggressive with guests and a little too comfortable pushing them around.

We're supposed to scare people, not grievously injure them, which has happened once or twice before. I really think we may have hired baby serial killers looking to get in some practice. Good thing they're easy to spot, always asking too many weird questions about the legality of what we do. Wanting to make sure that if they should just happen to slip up and really stab, maim, or kill somebody, they won't get in trouble. That's when I ask if they understand that murder is bad, illegal, and not permitted at all. Yes, we can push and shove and scream and use props to scare people, but we don't actually hurt anybody on purpose. Scraped knees and twisted ankles kind of come with the territory, but I called the cops on a dude who came on board as a runner. His only job was to sprint down Path #3 and scream at the top of his lungs while trailing his fake severed arm behind him. He took it upon himself to grab one of the guests and tie her up in the boathouse. The Groton sheriff came out here and escorted him off the property right in the middle of a game.

I had one new hire earlier in the season tell me that "technically" if someone runs into his knife, it's not murder. I cut him loose immediately.

And then there's staff like Heather and Jordan. Too busy doing freak-nasty stuff in the old arts-and-crafts building to do their jobs, then just bailing whenever they feel like it. We've lost three full-time staff members this season alone.

ME: I'll call some friends in the morning and see if they can come up and help us out

KYLE: Should we call Mr. Lamont?

Mr. Lamont owns Camp Mirror Lake, and while he never bothers to come out here and do any actual work, he does like to micromanage things over the phone.

ME: No. We can handle the last few nights ourselves. I'll call him after the season's over and let him know we'll need to bring on some more people for next summer.

No big deal.

KYLE: Ok. Cool.

I think for a moment.

ME: Hey. Were you trying to scare me in the showers just now? I went over there and it was already unlocked.

There is a long pause. I check the signal—two bars. Finally, my phone buzzes.

KYLE: Come on now. I'd never do that to you. This job getting to you, Charity?

ME: Shut up lol You think I'm scared?

KYLE: Me, you, and Tasha are the only Black folks here. Horror movies say we should be dead by now.

ME: I'm the final girl, boo. I will survive no matter what. It's my job.

Kyle texts me a series of butcher knife emojis and a meme of Michael Myers trying to grab Jamie Lee Curtis while she cowers in a closet.

ME: Jamie Lee is the ultimate final girl. Right behind Neve Campbell. Michael Myers can choke.

I've been a fan of horror movies and scary stories my whole life. I've read every Tananarive Due novel, seen every Jordan Peele film. I love horror movies even when everybody else thinks they're garbage. I will gladly debate anybody who got something to say about the masterpiece that is *Crimson Peak*. So when Rob shoved the job advertisement in my face and forced me to call the number for an interview, I jumped at the chance to be involved in the Camp Mirror Lake experience. I'm not scared of much, but I also know when not to press my luck. This job isn't getting to me, but walking into the unlocked community showers, which are supposed to be locked, while my flashlight is acting up? No, ma'am. Absolutely not.

I say good night to Kyle and put my phone back on the charger. I double-check my door and the two windows on my cabin to make sure everything is locked up. As I cut out the light and slip into bed, I can't help but wonder how we're going to manage shutting everything down for the season with a bare-bones staff.

There's a gust of wind, and the single light on the outside of my cabin flickers. I grip my Mace and slide my flashlight closer to me on the bedside table. Another gust rattles the entire cabin, and I pull the covers up to my neck, sinking into the bed, hoping that the slight sway in my curtains is just the wind pushing through a crack in the siding.

I smile. That is exactly what the people in horror movies say right before a dude with a hook for a hand jumps out and tears them apart.

It's just the wind.

There's nobody in the closet.

There is no one under the bed.

It's just your imagination.

CHAPTER 2

I'm lying in bed looking up at the crossbeams of my cabin ceiling. Why I'm awake, I have no idea. I glance at my phone. There are still thirty minutes left before my alarm goes off, but something has roused me from what I assume was a pretty deep sleep, judging by the drool on my pillowcase.

I sit up. The sun's just now cresting over a horizon I can't see, but the light is trickling through my window. I hear something—a splash in the lake directly across from my cabin. I'm out of bed and at the window in a blink.

A light layer of dew has laid itself across the ground during the night, and the dappled morning sunlight is making it sparkle. It should add to the faraway feel of this place, to a setting that, when we're not engaged in the game, should feel idyllic—but there is always the lake. It's the backdrop of this place, and no matter how hard I try, I can never quite force myself to think of it as anything other than foreboding. Upstate New York is filled with lakes, but this one makes my skin crawl every time I look at it.

The splash sounds again.

I huff. I know I have to check it out even though I don't want to. Part of my job is keeping everybody in camp terrified but generally safe, and that means making sure nobody is out there disobeying our very strict no-swimming rule.

On the porch, it's so humid I feel like I'm inhaling the mist from a boiling pot of water. Everything is damp and sticky and the insects love that. There is a never-ending parade of flies, gnats, and mosquitos that drives me nuts. I keep a can of Raid in my cabin for the times when the buzzing is too much to handle. Outside, a cloud of flies and mosquitoes is swarming the light bulb.

Nobody is supposed to be messing around in the lake. We have paddleboats and canoes, but they're just for looks. Their setup replicates the opening shot of *The Curse of Camp Mirror Lake* with the canoes bobbing in the water and the paddleboats nestled by the dock. It's perfect for the game. It makes the guests feel like everything is normal right before it all gets turned upside down.

The lake is flat calm this morning. Like a big sheet of black glass. I scan the area to see if maybe something has fallen in—a deer, a raccoon—but I don't see anything or anyone. Everything is still. I sigh and grab my phone, switch off the alarm. There's no sense in trying to get back to sleep.

I scroll through my emails, which haven't updated in a few hours due to the awful cell reception. The mini AC unit in my cabin is fighting for its life, so I switch it off and grab my shower kit and head over to the community stalls to clean up.

In the light of day, there's nothing to be afraid of. The shower building is a little run-down and the stalls are narrow, but the water's warm and I feel like a brand-new person after cleaning off the mess from the previous night's game.

I dress for the heat—shorts, T-shirt, sneakers—and as I make my way to the office cabin, the dew is already beginning to evaporate as the sun tilts through the towering pines. A layer of mist rises from the ground and billows around my ankles like a low-lying cloud.

Before I head to the main office, I do a walk-through of the camp to make sure everything is as it should be. I start at the eastern edge where the control center, located in the Craftsman Lodge, is situated. The outer door is locked, and I don't bother to check inside. There's never any issue in there, but outside, the generator is sitting like a relic from some bygone era. It broke last summer, and when I googled the make and model to see if I could fix it myself, it said it was built in 1990. I flip open the side panel. The fuel indicator reads full, and the little green light in the corner is steady, which means it's ready to kick on in case the main power fails. A good final girl always makes sure the generator, no matter how ancient, has fuel and is in good working order.

I cut through the wooded pathway between my cabin and

the shower building and come upon Porter and Javier, one of our new hires, arguing in a small clearing.

Porter's got his hand pushed down on his hip. "Just because you're too scared to go over there and check don't mean it doesn't need to be done."

"You do it, then," Javier says. "You know the whole place like the back of your hand. Doesn't it make more sense for you to go check?"

Porter throws his hands up, then spots me walking toward them.

"Oh, good," he says, clapping his hands together. "Boss is here. Let her tell you whose job it is to check the perimeter fencing because news flash, sugafoot, it ain't me."

I approach Javier. "That would be your job. Is there a problem?"

Javier smiles, and his right eyebrow arches up. He's tall, dark hair and eyes, a scattering of freckles across his cheeks and nose. He looks like an athlete, but I've seen him trip over damn near every exposed root or uneven pathway out here. I don't think he's coordinated enough to walk in a straight line, much less play sports.

"Aw, come on, Charity," he whines. "Porter is so much better at this. He knows every inch of this place, and besides, something might happen to me, and then we'd never get a chance to really know each other, you know?" He flashes me another smile. He's so obvious, it's actually a little funny.

"I'm a vegetarian," I say to him.

He looks at me, confused. "Huh?"

"She don't like meat," Porter says. "Strictly strawberries, like my man Harry Styles said."

Javier's brows push together. Me and Porter are both part of the alphabet mafia, so we get it, but poor Javier is clueless.

"I'm gay," I say. "Very, very gay. Save all that flirting and goofy grinning for somebody who wants it and who also isn't your direct supervisor."

Porter tilts his head to the side. "I, however, am strictly dickly and not your supervisor, so please feel free to try and seduce me. It probably still won't work because you're out here tryna hand your job duties off to somebody else, but I think you should give it a try anyway."

Javier looks like he might actually take Porter up on his offer, but I cut him off. "Javier, you gotta get on the perimeter check. It's important."

It still feels a little weird handing out tasks and staying on top of people's assigned jobs.

My previous two seasons, I always took on extra tasks— coordinated the game and set up reservations. I even worked to perfect our fake-blood recipes. At the start of this season, Mr. Lamont told me he was so impressed with my work ethic the previous summers that he was handing me the reins when it came to the day-to-day operations. He said I was responsible, self-sufficient, and trustworthy. That's mostly true. I'm all those things, but mostly because I don't have any other choices. Being the child of an irresponsible parent who doesn't really care what you're doing as long as it doesn't mess up her plans will do that to you.

Javier crosses his arms over his chest and huffs.

"Javi, it's literally in your job description," I say firmly. "And we all help out with it. You only have to do the check along the south side of the camp."

"Oh, okay," he says sarcastically. "Just the part of the fence that's right up against the darkest part of the woods. It's dark over there even in the daytime."

I glance toward the south side of the camp. He's not wrong, I guess. It's not that there are any less trees surrounding the other parts of camp; it's that the ones on the south side seem closer together. Like they're all crowding in on one another.

I sigh and turn back to Javier. "It's gotta get done, and it's on your to-do list, so please just get it done."

"Fine," Javier says. He looks around, then turns and walks toward the lake.

"Turn around," Porter says. "South is that way." He gestures toward the line of towering pine trees that crowd the space between the camp and the fencing that runs the entire length of the perimeter.

"I knew that," Javier says. He sucks in a big breath and lets it hiss out from between his teeth. "Okay. If I'm not in the office in twenty minutes, come find me because I'm lost."

Porter waves as Javier disappears into the tree line. As soon as he's out of sight, Porter turns to me. "Charity, we gotta stop bringing on these simple-ass mofos."

"Stop," I say, trying to hold in my laughter. "He's not that bad."

"He's pretty," Porter says, raising one perfectly arched brow and biting his bottom lip. "Very easy to look at, but looks aren't everything. You know what started our little back-and-forth?"

I shrug as we make our way toward the main lodge.

"He told me he was hoping to see a jackalope out here."

"A what?" I ask, confused. I'm familiar with most of the wildlife we get out here, but I've never heard of a jackalope.

Porter clasps the bridge of his nose between his fingers. "It's a rabbit with antlers . . . not a real thing." He sighs. "We need to run a perimeter check and make sure we're good to go for the biggest game of the summer, and this beautiful dummy is out here looking for mythological creatures."

"Maybe he was joking," I say.

Porter shakes his head. "Nah. He was dead serious, and that's why I'm concerned."

"Yikes," I say as we approach the arts-and-crafts lodge. "Did you tell him it's not real?"

Porter's fighting back a smile. "Yeah. He wasn't tryna hear it." He bends down and dusts some grass off the top of his shoe.

He's got on a brand-new pair of red sneakers with a reflective yellow swoosh on the side.

"Those are nice," I say. "Why are you wearing brand-new shoes out here? They're gonna get messed up so fast."

"Gotta keep it cute," he says. "Even if I do get sliced and

diced later on. I told Kyle to make sure he doesn't get any fake blood on me while he's stabbing me."

"How's that gonna work?" I ask.

Porter slings his arm around my shoulders. "By the time I die, most of the guests are so scared, they don't even notice the fake blood."

Porter and I have become close friends since last season. It's nice having somebody I can rely on when so many of the staff seem to just come and go, but beyond that, it feels good to have somebody to talk to about other stuff. Porter's dad is kind of a dick, too, so we understand each other in a way that not everyone else does.

"Okay," I say. "I want to double-check the hatch in the arts-and-crafts lodge." I look over my checklist of things I need to do. "It was sticking last night."

Porter follows me inside the arts-and-crafts building. It used to be a regular cabin, but now we use it to make props and test new ideas. We call it the arts-and-crafts lodge because calling it the fake-blood-and-murder-weapons test area doesn't have the same ring to it. We go to the hatch in the floor near the center of the room. It looks like any other part of the wood flooring, but there's one plank that's thinner than the others. It's a hidden pull, and when I flip it up and open the hatch, a loud groan cuts through the air.

"See," I say. "It only made a little bit of noise when Kyle popped up on the guests who were hiding in here. Now it sounds like the brakes on a train. We gotta do something about that."

Porter makes a note on a little pad of paper he keeps in his pocket. I smile. Besides the fact that I like Porter as a person, he's probably the best hire we've ever made. He made a point to study the camp inside and out, especially the trails, and he knows them better than any of us, which is helpful when you're trying to organize a game that takes place over all the acreage the camp sits on.

Porter and I finish up our check of the hatch and head to the office by the main entrance. As we pass Mirror Lake, I catch a glimpse of Tasha standing on the dock, peering down into the water. She's holding the pool skimmer we use to fish dead animals out of the lake.

"Tasha!" I yell. "You good?"

She glances back and grins. "Yeah! Just thought I heard something. Thought it was a opossum or something that fell in."

"Is it?" I ask. "Can you tell?" I recall hearing the splash in the lake, and now I'm worried we're gonna have a bunch of dead forest animals bobbing in the murky water.

"Not really," she says. "It's hard to see, though. I think there's something down there, but the skimmer's too short. Poor thing, whatever it is." She shakes her head, then catches a glimpse of Porter. "I see you, Porter! Your little hoochie-daddy shorts are real cute! You looking for a boyfriend out in these woods?"

Porter sticks out his leg, flexes his chiseled thigh, and grins. "I was tryna get Javier, but I think he's still stuck on you," Porter calls back.

Tasha laughs. She and Javier have been flirting so much, it's actually a little annoying. Like, hook up or knock it off.

As I scan the rocky shore of Mirror Lake, I catch a glimpse of something reflecting the early-morning sun. I jog over and scoop it up. It's a key chain with two keys attached and a little chain that says, TOWN OF GROTON, ESTD. 1817, in flaking white letters.

Porter joins me and peers over my shoulder. "More keys?"

I nod and shove them in my pocket.

Porter and I go into the main office to find a group of four people crowding the desk as a bewildered-looking Kyle flips through the reservation book while seated on a low stool.

"I just—what was your name again?" he asks, clearly flustered.

One girl with a long, dark braid down her back rolls her eyes and sticks out her neck. "Kennedy. *K-E-N-N—*"

"I know how to spell it," Kyle says. "Thanks."

I slide behind the desk and gently take the reservation book from him. He squeezes my shoulder and pushes the stool back from the counter. He starts to stand up, but I gently push him back down. He gives me a nod, and I turn my attention back to the woman on the other side of the desk.

"Reservation for Kennedy," I say, finding the name scrawled halfway down the page. "Four players. You'll be at the Crow's Nest, Cabin Two. You're all paid up. I can walk you to your daytime lodgings if you'd like to wait for me outside."

The girl grins. "Thank you." She shoots Kyle a smug little

smile. "At least somebody around here knows what they're doing." She and her friends leave, and I turn to look at Kyle.

"Pencil in the brunette to die in the woodshed," I say. "That'll scare the shit out of her."

Kyle smiles, and when he's sure no one can see him, he stands up. It'd be hard to keep up the illusion that a six-foot-eight serial killer is out to get you when the six-foot-eight dude at the desk is fumbling with paperwork and reservations. People can put two and two together sometimes, and it ruins the fun.

I crane my neck to look up at him. His big brown eyes are distant. I gently squeeze his arm. "Where is Felix anyway? He's supposed to be running the desk. You're not even supposed to be out here right now."

"I know," Kyle says. "But I saw those people come up the drive, and they were just standing around. The door was locked. Felix didn't even come in at all."

I glance around. The curtains are still drawn, the trash can is full, and the sign on the door is still turned to CLOSED. I rub my left temple. "Probably another no-show. We're having the worst luck this year."

Jordan and Heather, who play Victim #2 and Victim #3, had apparently already dipped out for the season, and now Felix is gone too. There are only three terror simulations left, including the big show on the final night of the season, and it's the worst time for staff members to be dropping like flies.

"These people are the only ones penciled in for tonight's

game, so we'll need anybody who's still here to play the other roles," I say. "We need to at least make it seem like there are other guests besides them. Do we have enough people for that?"

Staff coverage is dependent on the number of guests. The more guests there are, the less staff members are needed to play "real" victims. When the guest groups are large, we don't have to play double roles or take on other duties. We can focus on keeping them on the right paths and making sure they run into all our special-effects setups. Usually, it's me and my team of seven running the show and it works really well. It's a game, but it's a well-orchestrated one that feels a little too real when things run smoothly. Tonight, it's a small group, and we're short-staffed by three. Porter, Tasha, and Javier will have to pull double duty, working the sound system as well as being runners. I make a note to cuss out Felix, Jordan, and Heather the next time I see them. Professionally, of course. Very professionally cuss them out.

Kyle thinks for a moment. "We can pull it off. It'll be tough but yeah. We should be able to handle it."

"Okay. Let me go take this group to their cabin, and then we can start setting up. But hey." I lean toward Kyle. "Can you go check Felix's cabin and confirm he's not there?"

"Yeah, sure," he says. "He's bunking with Jordan and Heather, right?"

I nod. They were friends before they came to work here, so they decided to set up in the big cabin on the western side of camp. "Just make sure they're not laid out in there or something."

I take out my phone and send a text to the staff group chat asking Felix, Heather, and Jordan to at least let me know that they're definitely not coming back, but the text just sits there with a red exclamation point next to it, letting me know that it's not sent.

Kyle lumbers off, and I transfer the set of keys I found by the lake to a bucket in the cabinet behind the desk. I find all kinds of stuff on the lakeshore—keys, sunglasses, canteens. Most of it gets chucked in the trash, but I like to collect the keys. The jar under the counter is almost full after three summers.

I go outside to walk the group of players to their daytime lodgings. Most people like to check in, have a few drinks, and tour the actual cabins used in *The Curse of Camp Mirror Lake* before the game starts. Only staff actually stay through the entire night.

Leading the guests along the southern shore of Mirror Lake, past the boating and swim piers, we pass my cabin along the way, and I notice that I've left my porch light on, its thready light flickering. I sigh. The electricity better not act up. That's the last thing I need.

"You've all signed your waivers, but I'm required by law to state the terms out loud and get verbal agreements from all of you," I say. It's not true. But pretending like it's important adds another layer of fear to an already tense situation. "Camp Mirror Lake is a full-contact terror-simulation experience," I continue as we pass the other staff cabins. "Our staff are allowed to push you, shove you, scream at you, even restrain you."

"Wait," the brunette says, stopping in her tracks. "Restrain us? What does that even mean?"

I glance over my shoulder at her. "We can tie you up with rope or fabric restraints. No handcuffs and we can't cover your mouth or nose. We can blindfold you, though. So keep that in mind."

She doesn't ask any other questions as her friends laugh behind their hands.

A younger guy in a black T-shirt chuckles to himself. "This is so stupid. I don't know why I let y'all talk me into this."

"This camp was established to celebrate the 1983 cult horror classic *The Curse of Camp Mirror Lake*," I say, taking full offense. "They shot the movie on these very grounds, and we do our best to re-create the key events from the film."

"So if we've seen the movie, we should be all right?" one of the other guys asks. "We'll already know what's gonna happen?"

"No," I answer. "We change things up a little." We change things up a lot, actually. But it's always fun when the players think watching the movie will give them a leg up.

We approach the Crow's Nest lodging area, and I point out Cabin #2, a log structure with a green metal roof and a brick chimney.

"Meet your fellow players in the Western Lodge at eight to start the game." I hand the brunette the key to Cabin #2. "Hope you all survive the night." As I leave them to settle in, I make an executive decision. Tonight, there will be no survivors.

· · ·

The guests from Cabin #2, alongside Porter and Tasha posing as other real players, file into the Western Lodge a little before seven. I'm already there. I say hi to them, keeping my head down, making myself as small and invisible as possible. The wig helps. So does the makeup. The brunette doesn't even recognize that I'm the same girl who checked her in and took her to her cabin. Normally, Felix would do that, and I wouldn't meet the guests until we all get together in the main lodge. I'm still pissed about that, but I set it aside and focus on the task in front of me. I gently touch the back of my sweater, making sure the battery pack for my earpiece is concealed.

I tell the guests my name is Jade and that I'm so excited to be here at Camp Mirror Lake in a southern accent I borrow from my late grandmother. They latch on to my enthusiasm. I watch their eyes brighten, their mouths draw up. The excitement builds like water behind a dam. Everyone is buzzing around the big fireplace as I steal a quick glance at the clock on the wall. It's 7:59. There's a rustle of static across the line as my earpiece clicks on.

"It's go time," Kyle's voice says. "Remember, Charity says tonight is a no-survivors scenario. Everybody goes down." He laughs into the mic. "This is my favorite type of game."

Normally, we let a few guests slip through. We let them see the carnage, give them a few near-misses with Kyle, but ultimately somebody is left to accompany me to the front gates and claim their T-shirt at midnight. But not tonight.

The eight o'clock hour dawns. Staff Player #2, who is supposed to be Heather but is now being played by Javier, rushes in, limping slightly, covered in blood. He looks great, and I have to mask the flood of excitement I feel as the dam bursts and the rush of excitement overwhelms me. I always feel this way as the game commences, and the high is dizzying. My single complaint is that the fake blood he's drenched in is too opaque. I like it better when I can see through it just a little.

"Please!" Javier screams as he clings to the doorjamb, chest heaving. "Please help me! He—he's out there!"

"Who?" I ask. "What are you talking about?" I know my lines as well as I know my own name.

"A guy in a mask!" Javier bellows, real tears glinting in his eyes. "Help me!"

The brunette gasps as she clings to her friend, her eyes wide, her mouth halfway open. She's terrified. Only me and the remaining staff know that it's about to get a lot worse for her specifically. The rude guests are always the ones who end up crying or pissing their pants first.

Over the course of the next few hours, the guests move through a carefully curated series of experiences. I like to make sure they have a good view of Kyle in his mask, machete in hand, as he carves up Javier, Porter, and Tasha one by one. Of course we leave time for guests to "hide" or try to make their own plans for navigating the camp, but it's all a part of the game even if they don't realize it.

Halfway through the game, the guests end up separating, and Javier and Tasha have to herd them back to a common area so that we can move them toward the next gruesome display.

While they handle that, I find myself alone by the lake. I separate from the group early in the game so I can help with other special effects. I'm waiting for my cue, which, for tonight's game, is the audio of a girl screaming at the top of her lungs played over the tiny speakers hidden in the trees near the guest cabins. When it sounds, my job is to dump a bucket of fake blood mixed with a few pieces of raw chicken onto the path so the guests come across it.

As I wait in the shadow of a towering pine tree near Mirror Lake's shore, there's a splash in the water behind me. I turn to look, expecting to see one of the guests doing something they're not supposed to be doing, but there's no one.

I take a step toward the lake.

Just offshore, I spot something in the water. A shadowy human-size shape bobbing near the surface. Their head and shoulders move up and down, but I can't see their face.

"Hey!" I shout. "Get out of there! You can't be in the water!" I edge my way along the shore. Who the hell is out there? Who'd want to be? "Hey!" I shout again.

"Charity, go!" A voice sounds in my earpiece, and my heart jumps into my throat.

I scramble back to the path and spill the bucket of blood and raw chicken across the dirt. In the dark, it looks like somebody has met a grisly end right there, and as I hide in the shrubbery, gasps and terrified whispers erupt from the guests as they come across it.

As their voices fade, I turn back to the lake. It's silent now, and I'm worried. I rush to the shore, as close to the last location of the person as I can get.

I touch my earpiece. "Can I get a head count for the guests? Like, right now."

As I wait for a response, I peer into the dark water. I can still see . . . something. A dark shape just below the surface. I sprint to the lifeguard tower, which, again, is just for decoration but is accurate right down to the bright orange life preserver draped over the perch at the top.

I scramble up the rickety structure and yank the ring down and tuck it under my arm. I jump down and rush back to the lake, tossing the ring in right where the person went under the water.

"Charity." Javier's voice cuts through the static in my earpiece. "All the guests are accounted for. All four of them are here."

A wave of relief rushes over me, and I heave an exasperated sigh. I stare into the water. The dark shape is gone. The only movement is coming from the life preserver floating atop the water.

CHAPTER 3

"The trapdoor in the arts-and-crafts lodge is still sticking," I say as I check my notes the following day at our morning meeting. "Anybody have any suggestions on how to fix it?"

"Have we tried WD-40?" Porter offers.

Javier closes the curtains in the main lodge, trying to keep the light from the rising sun from accosting us. "What's WD-40?" he asks.

"It's, like, some kind of grease or oil for hinges," Porter says. "Keeps them from sticking. My dad uses it on stuff around the house all the time."

"I'll check the supply shed, but I don't think I've seen anything like that," I say as I sink into the ratty old couch in the Western Lodge. The seat is so low, I'm almost touching the floor. It used to have a trundle underneath that kept the middle from sinking in, but during a game a few weeks ago, some of the guests thought it'd be funny to use it as a raft on the lake. Now there's just a big open space under the couch that comes in handy if we need a quick place to hide during the game but sucks when you forget about the empty space, dive into the couch after a long day, and almost break your tailbone in half on the floor. I check my to-do list, which is growing longer by the minute. I have a headache just thinking about how difficult that's going to be when we're so short-staffed.

"Where the hell is everybody?" Javier asks. "They just dipped? Real professional."

"Oh, right," Kyle says, turning to me. "That reminds me. I went over to the big cabin and knocked. Nobody answered. I looked inside. It's a mess in there, bunch of trash and stuff lying around, but they're not in there."

I'm irritated that Jordan, Heather, and Felix left a mess behind for the rest of us to clean up. "Yeah, they're no-shows," I say, rubbing my temple. "That means it's just the five of us for tonight's game and the big show tomorrow night and . . ." I hesitate. Nobody is going to want to hear the next part. "And listen, after the final game, I need everybody to stick around and help close down the camp."

"Huh?" Porter asks. "Wait, wait, wait. Nobody said anything about staying past closing night."

"I know," I say. "Heather and Jordan volunteered, but since they're MIA, somebody has to do it. I'm staying, too, of course. If we all pitch in, it'll take maybe two days max."

Javier shakes his head. "Nope. I got plans."

Tasha scoots closer to Javier and nudges him with her shoulder. "You sure you gotta go?"

Javier smiles, and his eyebrows shoot up his forehead. "Uh. I mean, no. I guess not."

"What plans do you have anyway, Javier?" Kyle asks. "Hanging out with your grandma?"

The smile is gone from Javier's face immediately. "Yeah. So?" Javier tilts his head to the side. "She's good company. And she can cook." He puts his hand on Tasha's leg, and Porter rolls his eyes. "I can stay," Javier says. "But I think there's some squirrels living in the wall of my cabin. Can we do something about that?"

I add the issue to my laundry list of other things I need to tell Mr. Lamont about once I can actually get ahold of him. He leaves way too many of the responsibilities to me, and I hate it sometimes. I bite the end of my pen and try to think in a straight line. "It's too late to get any new people hired on, and I can't do this by myself. I'm inviting some of my friends up to help out."

I take my phone out and send a group text to my girlfriend, Bezi, and my friend Paige.

ME: Do yall want to come up to the camp for a few days? Bezi, I know you were gonna pick me up anyway but can you come up a few days early? I can comp you a cabin and maybe yall can help me fill in a few of the "victim" roles? I'm short staffed.

PAIGE: I'm in.

Three little dots pop up and then disappear, as if Bezi is typing and erasing a response.

Bezi is big on outdoor stuff. She loves the camp setting, but she hates that Mr. Lamont is running the Camp Mirror Lake game out here. She thinks it's weird, and if I'm being honest, she's not wrong. Mr. Lamont's motivations for running the camp are clear—he loves money and the attention that the camp gets even when it's not always positive.

Bezi's response pops up a moment later.

BEZI: Sure, babe. Hey Paige . . . be ready when I pull up because I am not waiting around. I know you like to take your sweet time.

PAIGE: Whatever Bezi. Don't rush me!

ME: If yall get here soon enough you can play tonight's game.

PAIGE: I'm about to be so dramatic. Like, over the top dramatic Just FYI

BEZI: ok

ME: See yall soon then

I attempt to send another message to Bezi to let her know I'm not gonna make her do anything she doesn't want to do, but all my bars disappear. I wait, and after a few moments, there's still no signal, so I slip my phone back in my pocket. "Two of my friends are coming up to help out. Do any of you have someone you can call?"

Javier, Kyle, and Porter all shake their heads.

"I'd call you or Paige or Bezi," Tasha says. "But I'm guessing you already asked them."

I nod. Bezi, Tasha, Paige, and I have been like family since the sixth grade, and Tasha is just as close to them as I am.

"I'll figure it out," I say.

"Shouldn't Mr. Lamont be the one figuring this stuff out?" Porter asks. "He's the owner. He should be worrying about this, not you, Charity."

I sigh and sink deeper into the couch. Mr. Lamont loves to micromanage, but he doesn't want to actually do any work. He almost never comes into camp, but he loves to leave lists and ideas about how to make the camp scarier. One area that he's knee-deep in is bringing on new people. He insists on approving all new hires, but he's bad at answering his phone or replying to messages. Sometimes, even when I find a good candidate, he takes forever to get back to me and the person just moves on.

I check my phone, and the signal is still trash. My call to Mr. Lamont fails immediately. "I'm gonna go call him from the office," I say, standing up. "Let's just keep this rickety shit together for tonight and tomorrow; then we'll shut it down and get out of here, okay?"

Kyle gives a slight nod. He'll probably stick around and so will Tasha, but both Javier and Porter avoid looking me directly in the eye.

I leave them and make my way to the main office. It's locked up tight, just the way I'd left it the previous night, which means Felix is definitely done for the season. I remember looking at his employment application and calling his references for Mr. Lamont. "Punctual" was one of the words his previous employers had used to describe him. I roll my eyes and just shake my head.

I scan the parking lot from the small deck outside the office. No vehicles except for the Camp Mirror Lake pickup truck that we use to drive the forty minutes to the little town of Groton for groceries and other supplies. It's as unreliable as Heather, Jordan, and Felix. Last time I drove it, it turned off right in the middle of the narrow two-lane road that leads up to the camp. I had to steer it onto the nonexistent shoulder and walk the rest of the way. Mr. Lamont had it towed back to camp, but I don't think he actually got it fixed.

I unlock the office, flip the sign to OPEN, and go in to call Mr. Lamont on the landline. The phone looks like something out of some bad nineties movie, and even though I'm used to it, a lot of people my age have never had the opportunity to hear a dial tone before making a call. I dial Mr. Lamont's number. It rings and rings until his voice mail picks up.

"Leave a message," Mr. Lamont's voice grumbles on the recording just before a screeching tone sounds in my ear.

"Uh, hi, Mr. Lamont. It's Charity. Listen, we've had a bunch of no-shows, and I'm running on a skeleton crew. I think we can handle the game tonight and tomorrow, but we need to talk about who we're bringing on next season. Turnover is always high, and there's always one person who just up and quits mid-season, but Felix, Heather, and Jordan are all no-shows. I don't know, maybe you could come up for a while? Maybe having an adult around would be a good idea?" I sigh. "Call me here on my cell phone when you get a minute. You know how bad the signal is out here so just leave me a message if you can't get through. Thanks."

I sit the receiver back in the cradle and check the reservation book. One group of six people is paid up, and a little spark of excitement courses through me. A big group is always more fun. I pencil their names into the game roster alongside the remaining staff and my friends. Paige is a horror-movie stan, so I jot down her name under Staff Victim #1. She'll love that. I'll stick Bezi on audio-visual duty, since she loves to watch people be scared but doesn't actually want to be scared herself.

. . .

I'd penciled myself in for blood duty in addition to my role as Final Girl. Blood duty is just as important as being the final girl. The game begins when a staff member busts into the lodge drenched in fake blood. It has to look authentic enough to pull the guests into the game.

I spend the morning making four batches of blood. I'm constantly adjusting the recipe, but so far the best combination has been Karo corn syrup as the base, then a few drops of red food coloring. On its own, it's nothing special, but the secret is adding a drop of yellow to the mix and one or two drops of green. Red food coloring alone makes the corn syrup too translucent. Bright red fake blood sounds nice, but in person it just looks cheap. It has to be a much darker red in order to look believable as it's dripping from the top of my head and down the side of my face at the end of the night.

I mix up a small batch and test the color by dipping a small brush into the bowl and dragging it across the back of my hand. The coloring is perfect, but it starts to bead up on my skin and that's a no-go. I search around under the counter until I find a bottle of clear dish soap. A few drops added to the blood mix keeps it from beading up, and after another test swatch, our fake blood is good to go for the night's game with enough to cover tomorrow's final game too. I haul two of the gallon-size containers into the walk-in fridge and leave the others out for later.

I check the prop room, which is less of a room and more like a narrow closet, that contains game-night props. The ax rig—a rubber knife hot glued to a harness—is nestled in among the imitation severed limbs. It's my favorite special effect because it can be positioned to look like a serial killer has embedded the weapon in your chest or in your back. It was my idea, and it looks great, especially in the dark. Alongside it are a few other rubber knives. Kyle likes to switch it up sometimes. We also have an assortment of latex body parts we grabbed from a thrift shop in town. We didn't ask why there was a bucket of fake body parts at the Salvation Army; we just bought them and worked them into the game. Nothing quite like tripping over a severed leg as Kyle bears down on you with a butcher knife.

Everything is in order and ready to go. I lock up the prop closet, but as I do, a noise drifts in on the warm breeze gusting through the cracked window at the front of the lodge. The crunching of gravel and the bass blowing out somebody's car speakers. I race to the parking lot as a car careens down the last part of the two-mile-long driveway that snakes up from the main road. Tasha emerges from the boathouse and is straightening out her shirt as Javier stumbles out behind her. He heads off toward the staff cabins as Tasha joins me in the parking lot.

"You good?" I ask, noticing her smudged lipstick and mussed hair.

Tasha grins and pulls her head full of tight coils up into a high pouf and secures it with a bright pink hair tie. "Yup."

I roll my eyes but can't keep from laughing a little. "You and Javier are a mess."

"I know," she says, still smiling. "I'm good with that."

Dust and gravel trail the car like a storm cloud as Bezi swings into a parking spot directly across from the office.

Paige hops out first. She squeals as she jogs up to me and grabs me in a bear hug. "I can't wait to scare the shit outta people, Charity. What role you got me playing?" She claps her hands together. "Tell me! I'm so excited!"

"You're Staff Victim Number One," I say, laughing. "You get to be stabbed."

She jumps up and down and gives me another squeeze. "I can't wait to write about this. I'm chronicling the whole thing for the school paper. When we start school in the fall, I'm leading with an exposé on this place. It's gonna be great! You're gonna get so much business!"

Paige and Tasha hug it out, and I turn to see Bezi crawling over the center console and stumbling out of the passenger side door.

I rush over and grab her hand. "What is goin' on here?"

Bezi shuts the door and laughs. "The driver side door won't open from the inside."

"It's a death trap," Paige says. "And you don't deserve to have a driver's license, Bezi."

"But did you die?" Bezi asks, a wicked little grin spreading across her face.

"No," Paige says. "I get to die later. I'm Staff Victim Number One! Imagine the headline." She holds her hands up in front of her like she's envisioning the words. "I Survived Camp Mirror Lake and All I Got Was This Crappy T-Shirt." She's got her camera dangling from her neck, and she lifts it, snapping a few shots of the entrance and the main office.

I shake my head. "Actually, no T-shirt for you, boo. Those are only for actual guests."

Paige pokes out her bottom lip and sighs. "Fine. As long as I get to have my picture taken with the fake ax and all the fake blood and stuff."

"Deal," I say.

Tasha comes over and slings her arm around my shoulders. "We gotta keep an eye on her," she whispers. "She be taking things a little too far sometimes."

Paige points her camera at Tasha, who immediately starts posing like she's some kind of supermodel.

Bezi wraps her arms around me. "Please tell me I don't have to get fake sliced up."

I pull her close to me. "You're gonna be on audio-visual duty because I know you're a big ol' scaredy-cat."

She laughs. She looks amazing—her broad smile, her waist-length braids trailing down her back—I can't help but stare at her. She's the only thing I really miss when I'm out here.

"Look at Paige's feet," she whispers against my ear.

I glance at Paige, who I just now realize is wearing Timbs, and I can't help but laugh.

"Did you for real wear Timbs to camp?"

Paige looks down at her feet. "They're work boots, Charity. They work in the snow at home; they can handle these little sticks and leaves y'all got out here."

"I'm just glad you're here," I say. "Really. Y'all are the real MVPs."

"We got you, babe," Bezi says, slipping her arm around my waist. "But in between slicing campers up and all that, I want to take some pictures."

"I got pictures covered," Paige says, giving her camera a little shake.

"I know you're gonna take pictures for your story, but I want to take some for myself. I love it out here; I just hate—" She stops short. Bezi leans against my shoulder. "You know what people say about this place."

I pretend to be shocked. "What do you mean, Bezi? What could people possibly be saying about this magical place?"

Bezi rolls her eyes, but she's still smiling. "Okay, okay. You don't have to be so sarcastic."

I pull her in and kiss her cheek.

"They say the lake's haunted," Bezi says as her gaze drifts toward the water.

"Who is *they*?" I ask.

Bezi shrugs. "You know, people. People in town."

I know what people say. Beyond the rumors about the terror simulation itself, there are other things. I can't deny that the entire camp can feel a little heavy sometimes. Like something's hanging over it, but I mostly feel like that's because we pretend to murder people out here on a nightly basis. Unease is kind of the goal. Strange occurrences at the lake are fodder for all kinds of wildly overexaggerated stories. There are old stories about a creature in the lake. Something like the Loch Ness Monster but on a smaller scale. All the lakes in upstate New York are supposedly full of monstrous beasts, but they only show up in blurry cell phone footage or pictures that look like they were taken with the first camera ever made.

There are all kinds of stories about people drowning in the lake, which—it's a lake. Accidents happen. It's tragic, of course, but that doesn't mean it's haunted. And the drownings have been documented, but so has the fact that lots of those people were way too drunk to have been swimming in the first place. There were other stories too. Things that don't fit nicely with the narrative that most of the deaths at the lake were because of bad luck or poor choices. Sometimes backpackers coming through the camp in the off season claim to have seen shadowy figures on the shore or sometimes in the water. I shake my head and push those thoughts away. Still, I had seen . . . something.

"All of that is just stuff people say, scary stories people tell around campfires," I reassure Bezi. "You know that, right?"

Bezi shrugs. "Do I?"

"They are," I say.

Bezi looks skeptical, and I don't know who I'm really trying to convince—her or me. Tasha and Paige trail us to the main office, and I grasp Bezi's hand in mine. "I'm the final girl. I'll keep you safe."

She grins. "If you're the final girl, what does that mean for the rest of us?"

"It means we're all dead," Tasha says, grinning.

• • •

The guests check in at five. It's a group of college-age guys, one of whom is clearly scared out of his mind before the game even starts. I overhear him say he's scared of the dark, the woods, water, bugs, and basically all wildlife. How his friends convinced him to come up here is beyond me, but I feel bad, so I decide to let him be one of the survivors. He can get a T-shirt and earn some bragging rights.

I go over the roles I've assigned to Paige and Bezi and

double-check that everyone else knows what they need to do for the night. Then Bezi and I walk over to the Camp Mirror Lake control center.

The security building is the nicest one at camp because it houses the only equipment worth anything in this entire place. There are speakers and cameras camouflaged throughout the camp, and whoever is on audio-visual duty for the night can cue up all kinds of effects: screams, footsteps, groans, even the sound of heavy breathing. The projectors that cast hulking shadows through the trees are some of the creepier effects.

We use the cameras to keep tabs on all the guests and make sure they're not veering too far off the beaten path. I don't have time to chase drunken frat boys through the woods in the middle of a game.

I open the padlock on the front door to the control room and pull it open. It's hot inside, so I flip on the little box fan in the corner as Bezi stations herself at the control panel.

"Here's the schedule," I say, handing her a binder that has all the timing for the special effects. "Staff watches are synced to that clock." I gesture to a digital clock mounted above the series of monitors and keyboards. "Everything is labeled, and the mic is connected directly to the headsets we wear during the game. Just press the buttons next to our names to talk to us individually or press the big red button to talk to all of us at once. Think you can handle it?"

She waves me away. "I got this. I get a front-row seat to all the scares without actually having to be involved? Yeah. Not a problem." She stands up and throws her arms around my neck and kisses me. "Is there a camera in here?" A little grin spreads across her lips.

"No," I say.

I run my hands up her back and breathe her in. She kisses me, and I let my fingers trail over her arms and up the sides of her neck. I've missed her. A lot.

I'm at the camp for weeks during the summer with no breaks, but she understands. Bezi knows I'd rather be anywhere other than at home, where my mom and Rob are busy forgetting, or maybe regretting, that I exist. When I go home at the end of the season, Rob always acts surprised to see me. Like he's hoping one day I just won't come home at all.

It wasn't always like that, but now it's all there is. Sometimes I wish the camp would run year-round just so I never have to go home. Most of the time when I'm up here, my mom doesn't even call to check on me. Not that she'd be guaranteed to get through with the signal being as bad as it is, but sometimes when I go into town, all the missed calls and voice mails from Bezi and Paige pop up at once. It's almost never my mom's number or voice on the other end.

I kiss Bezi, drowning out the ache of missing who my mom was before she decided she wasn't really into being a mom. Bezi playfully pushes me back, and I lose my footing, stumbling into a locked door that leads to a small room at the back of the cabin.

"Shit. Sorry, Charity." Bezi grabs my arm to steady me. "I got a little carried away. I miss you. Can you tell?"

"A little," I say, laughing.

Bezi tries to peer through the glass, but it's covered with yellowing newspaper that's been plastered on from the inside. "What's back there?" she asks.

"Nothing much. It's locked anyway."

"What if I need another way out?" Bezi asks.

"Oh, it's not an exit," I say. "It's a storage room that Mr. Lamont keeps locked up. It's just extra audio and visual equipment. He doesn't trust anybody around that stuff because of how expensive it is. I don't even have a key."

Bezi's brows push up. "I mean, a bunch of teenagers running a terror-simulation camp for weeks on end with no supervision? What's not to trust?"

That's the thing. Mr. Lamont knows that, legally, at least one adult is supposed to be here anytime there are minors working the camp, and while I'm just shy of my eighteenth birthday, that doesn't count. He always says it's fine and that nobody is going to ask too many questions, but just in case, he had me prepare a whole speech about how Mr. Lamont checks in once a day in person and is always a phone call away if I need him. It's a lie, of course, but Mr. Lamont pays me on time every week and in cash, so I don't mind covering for him.

"I gotta go get ready," I say, kissing Bezi again. "What look should I go for tonight? Braids or my Kim Kardashian wig?"

"Braids?" Bezi asks. "You have time to do that?"

"It's a wig. It's already braided up and everything."

Bezi presses her lips together. "Please tell me it's not one of them Tyler Perry wigs. I can't let you walk around like that."

"I mean, Madea's lace is always melted to the gods."

"And everybody else's wigs look like hot garbage."

"It's not *that* bad."

Bezi looks skeptical.

I laugh so hard, little tears roll out of my eyes. "I promise! It's not that bad, and even if it was, it'll be dark. Nobody will be able to tell it's not real."

Bezi points to the camera. "If I see you running through the woods lookin' like Omarion, I'm breaking up with you."

"Damn, really?" I say, laughing. I pull her close and kiss her again.

She presses her forehead against mine, and I can feel her heart pounding as she presses her body close to mine. "Okay. Maybe I won't break up with you, but I'll never forgive you for it."

"We can't just throw away two years together because of a bad wig," I say.

Bezi puckers her lips and raises her eyebrows. "You sure about that?"

I laugh, kiss her one more time, and then turn and head out the door to get ready.

"Hey, Charity," Bezi calls after me.

I glance back at her, and she narrows her eyes.

"Be careful," she says. "You know what happens to Black folks in slasher movies."

"I'm the final girl," I say. "Guaranteed to survive the night."

"You better," she says before closing the door.

CHAPTER 4

That night, as the clock strikes eight and the game begins, the remaining staff, alongside Bezi and Paige, play their roles to perfection. All the guests meet their gruesome "deaths" at the hands of Kyle's mask-wearing, machete-wielding alter ego. All except one. The young blond guy who was scared to death straight out of the gate. He started off by immediately abandoning his friends. Bezi was tracking him on the camera but then lost sight of him on the campgrounds for about thirty minutes. I don't find him until she cues up the phantom footsteps and he scrambles out from under a supply shed.

I'm leading him to the finish to let him know he's won. He stayed hidden and avoided Kyle the entire night. It's not necessary. I was gonna let him live regardless, but this guy hid for most of the game, and while his friends are probably gonna hate him for abandoning them, he's a special kind of winner—another final survivor. Just like me.

"Come on!" I yell frantically. "I—I think the people who work here took things too far! I'm really hurt!"

The guy stares wide-eyed at my arm as I hold it tight against my body, fake blood dripping off my fingertips.

"They can't do that!" he screams, his voice cracking. "Wait. Can they do that? Can they hurt you?"

"I—I don't know. I didn't think so." I clench my jaw and turn my face away from him so he doesn't see me smile. I'm usually super professional, playing my part to the very end, but this guy is so scared, I really do feel bad for him. I'm glad he's going to claim the prize of a shitty T-shirt and what is sure to be a hideous picture of himself emerging from under the Camp Mirror Lake signage.

We stumble down Path #3, past the campfire ring and the main office, past the parking lot with the beat-up camp truck, Bezi's car, and another one that belongs to the guests and Tasha's "lifeless" body. The prop ax is sticking out of her chest, and she's gone way overboard with the fake blood. It's going to take her forever to get it out of her hair and off her skin, but knowing Tasha, she's having the time of her life. In the darkness, I can't even see the rise and fall of her chest. She really looks dead.

I usher the last guest past her and under the big wooden sign, where we cling to the metal gate. I pause. I wait. Nothing happens.

"What—what do we do now?" the guy stammers.

I scan the tree line for Kyle. He should be making his way toward us from the opposite side of the gate by now. It takes me a minute to spot the darkened silhouette down the road. He's a little off his cue, but it's still workable.

"Oh no," I say, trying my best to sound desperate and terrified. "Oh no! Please!"

The figure moves closer, and I let my fingers dance over the handle of the fake butcher knife tucked in my waistband.

Just then, there is movement in the brush to my right.

I glance over, straining to see into the dark. Another figure—tall and hulking—is just beyond the tree line. My gaze darts between the two. My first thought is that one of the guests got turned around and somehow ended up outside the perimeter of the camp. But Bezi would have seen that, and she would have let me know. Some of the light from the parking lot filters through the trees, and I see that the figure to my right is Kyle. I turn my attention back to the figure in the road, and as they stalk forward, I take a step back from the gate. This is wrong. There's someone else in the game, and it's not someone I recognize. My heart kicks up.

"What's going on?" the blond guy asks.

Suddenly, the floodlights in the parking lot come up. They bathe the entire area in a brilliant white haze. The Halloween theme music begins to play, and the other staff and guests emerge from their holding areas.

"I want my damn money back!" yells one of the guests as he stalks up to the gate. "Supposed to be a serial killer out here, right? Whose grandma is this?" He gestures to the other side of the gate, and I realize the person approaching is an older woman in dingy coveralls and a flannel shirt. Her wispy gray hair is loose and falls over her face like a veil. In her right hand is something long and slender and double-barreled—a shotgun. Every muscle in my body tenses. I want to run, but I feel like I can't move.

Kyle suddenly ducks deeper into the woods and emerges behind us a few moments later, his mask now situated on top of his head. With trembling fingers, I touch my earpiece.

"Bezi?"

"Yeah." Her voice crackles in my ear. "Who is that at the entrance? Is that a player? Wait. Oh my god, Charity! She has a gun!"

"Open the mics and tell everybody to get inside and lock the doors," I say. "Now!"

Bezi's voice commands anyone not already at the front gate to get to the Western Lodge and lock themselves in. There's a flurry of panicked footsteps and shouts from behind me, but I don't take my eyes off the woman. She raises the gun and cradles it in the crook of her arm with the barrel pointing up to the sky.

"You think this is a game?" she asks, her voice low and gravelly. She narrows her eyes at me; then she turns and glances over her shoulder as if she's looking for someone behind her.

My mouth is suddenly dry. I try to stifle the fear that is pooling in my chest, but I can barely move. I force myself to take another step back.

"Everybody get inside the office!" I shout.

The guests, Porter, and Tasha retreat to the office. Kyle stays beside me, gripping his machete as if its rubber blade will do either one of us any good.

"This is my place. My land. All of it." The woman turns her head and spits on the ground. "You damn kids think you can do whatever you want out here? You think there won't be consequences?" As the woman rambles on, she keeps the shotgun in the crook of her arm. She touches her face with her free hand, then tilts her head back and laughs. "It's all fun and games, right? Pay to play? You should be ashamed. If you knew what I know . . ." She trails off, and her eyes glaze over.

"What are you talking about?" Kyle asks.

The woman's gaze flits to him. She suddenly rushes the front gate and sticks her hand through, grasping at the front of my shirt. I stumble back and fall into the dirt, but I'm back on my feet a half second later because there's no way in hell I'm going to trip over my own feet and twist my ankle. That's not what final girls do.

"Charity," Kyle says as he grips my arm and pulls me toward the office. "Look."

I glance at him, and his eyes are wide and filled with a kind of fear I've never seen in his expression before. He taps the breast pocket of his dingy jumpsuit, and in the glow of the floodlight, I can see the outline of the heavy padlock we use to keep the front gate secure while the game is being played.

He forgot to lock us in.

I glance at the woman just as she leans on the gate and it yawns open. A smile dances across her crooked mouth.

I'm running before I can think, my legs pumping under me, my chest heaving. Kyle is at my heels. We barrel toward the office, where Tasha is waiting with the door open.

"Get in here!" she screams.

I race up the steps and fall into the office as Kyle and Tasha slam the door shut and turn the dead bolt. A bang erupts from the outside as the woman crashes into the door. Her pinched face appears in the window. Backlit by the muted glow from the floodlight in the parking lot and the pitch-black night sky, she looks like she could play the killer in one of our nightly games. Her stringy gray hair obscures her face; the skin that's visible is loose and reminds me of weathered leather. Her thin lips pull back, exposing her teeth. She turns the shotgun around and bangs the butt of it against the glass.

"Little pig, little pig, let me come in," she hollers through a throat full of popping and snapping phlegm.

She can get in if she wants to. The lock on the door is old and wobbly in the frame, and even if that managed to stop her, she could probably kick hard enough to come through the wall. The office's exterior walls are so thin, I can hear her breathing and talking to herself outside.

"What is happening?" Porter asks in a terrified whisper-scream.

"Is this part of the game?" one of the guests asks.

"No!" I touch my earpiece. "Bezi! Lock the door to the control center! Do not come out!"

She says something, but I can't make it out through the static and over the rush of blood in my ears. Several of the guests have their phones out, but none of them can get a signal long enough to call or text for help.

"Use the landline," I say.

The woman paces back and forth on the porch, mumbling to herself and slamming her fist against the glass every few seconds, causing us all to jump out of our skin.

Porter calls the sheriff's office, and then we wait because the drive up here is something serious even when it's not pitch-dark outside. Nobody says anything. We barely even breathe. The woman's footsteps are heavy on the porch, and each time her weathered face bobs past the window, my heart cartwheels in my chest.

I turn away from the window and speak quietly into my mic again. "Bezi? Bezi, please answer me."

"I'm here," she finally whispers, and the relief that washes over me makes me dizzy. "Paige is in here with me. We're hiding in that old closet in the back. I thought you said there was just extra equipment in here."

A loud crack suddenly splits the air, and I instinctively duck as a wave of hushed cries ripples through the room. The woman has fired her gun into the air and is now grinning maniacally through the office window.

"We're gonna die," one of the guests says.

"Maybe we should rush her," Javier says.

"She has a shotgun," Porter says. "You can't be serious." He glares at Javier, then throws his hands up. "Never mind."

The woman continues to pace, switching her gun from one hand to the other. I keep my eyes glued to the window until finally, the red-and-blue haze from the sheriff's car cuts through the dark and lights up the shadowy forest.

Gravel crunches under his tires as the sheriff pulls into the main parking lot. I try to see how many cars are coming to the rescue, but I only see the one. Sheriff Lillard steps out and approaches the woman with his hands folded across his chest.

"Porter," I say. "Did you tell him she has a gun?"

"Yeah," Porter says. "Guess he doesn't care?"

"What are you doing out here, Nancy?" Sheriff Lillard asks. There is no concern in his voice at all.

I whip my head around and stare at Kyle. "He knows her?"

Kyle shrugs. "Sounds like it. Maybe she lives in town?"

I crane my neck to watch as Sheriff Lillard strolls right up to the woman he'd called Nancy. He pats her gently on the shoulder, then loops his arm under hers and escorts her to his squad car, gun in hand. She sits down in the back seat, and he says something to her that I can't make out through the door.

Once he closes the car door, I slide the dead bolt open and go out onto the front porch. Sheriff Lillard turns his back on the shotgun-wielding woman who's sitting uncuffed in his back seat.

"Are you all right?" he asks.

"No." I don't even know what kind of question that is. Am I all right after a strange woman threatened me with a shotgun? Yeah, no.

Sheriff Lillard pulls off his cap and runs his hand through

his sandy-blond hair. "I'm sorry about that. Miss Keane here gets a little territorial sometimes." He tugs at the back of his neck. "Can't really blame her."

Tasha appears at my side, her arms crossed, her expression angry. "What's that supposed to mean? We can absolutely blame her."

Sheriff Lillard stares at her, blinks, then allows a grin to slowly spread across his face.

"What's funny?" Tasha asks, clearly annoyed. "I don't see anything funny about this at all!"

I glance at her and realize she's still got the prop ax embedded in her chest, and the dried fake blood has stained her face and neck.

"Looks like somebody got to you before Miss Keane had a chance," Sheriff Lillard says, biting back a laugh. He clears his throat and replaces his cap.

The guests storm out of the office and brush past me.

"This is supposed to be fake!" one of them yells.

"It is!" I shout back.

The blond guy gets in his car and starts the engine. He looks like he's thinking about leaving his companions behind, but after the others retrieve their belongings from their cabin, they pile into the car and turn out of the parking lot.

"Aren't you gonna get statements from them or something?" I ask Sheriff Lillard. "They all saw what happened."

"Oh, I don't think that's necessary," he says as the guests take off down the road, a cloud of dust swirling behind them.

I jog down the stairs and stand in front of Sheriff Lillard. We've met twice before. First when he came up to the camp to introduce himself when I initially got hired. He told me he was just a phone call away in the event of an emergency. And the second time was when he arrested that staff member who got too carried away. Now he's looking at me like he doesn't recognize me.

"I'm Charity," I say, pulling off my wig. "I'm the manager here. I want—"

Recognition seems to wash over him, and he cuts me off mid-sentence. "Oh, right. You're that little girl Lamont's got running this shit show. You know he's supposed to be on premises, right?"

"He is," I lie. "He checks in every day. That's not what we're talking about, though."

Sheriff Lillard rolls his eyes. Our first interactions had been friendly enough, but now he seems oddly dismissive. Like he doesn't want to be up here even though a weird lady with a gun was threatening us. I have to take a second to check myself. I know full well that the police aren't here to protect and serve; they're here to enforce compliance with whatever set of rules they're following today.

"Shit show or not, are you gonna do anything about her?" I point to the woman. "She was waving that gun around, and she fired it into the air. I'm pretty sure that's illegal."

He glances over his shoulder at her. "Nancy. Tell me you weren't firing that thing around these kids."

Nancy opens the rear door of the police cruiser, and I realize

Sheriff Lillard didn't even close the door all the way. I have to clench my jaw to keep my mouth from falling open.

She shrugs and laughs a little. "Aw, hell. If I wanted to shoot them, I'd have done it."

"Then we'd have a real problem on our hands," Sheriff Lillard says sarcastically as he pulls at his neck. He sounds like every other backwoods law-enforcement official I've ever come across in Groton—way too sure of himself, glaring air of supremacy. I'm feeling all the stress of being under threat from the lady with the shotgun and the person who is supposed to at least be pretending to keep us safe. "I don't think we need to *do* anything," Sheriff Lillard says. "I'll probably take her home and make sure she gets some rest."

"Probably take her home?" I repeat, like the words don't make sense. I'm not surprised that this heffa is getting special treatment, but I *am* irritated. "She literally has a gun in her lap right now."

"We're in the woods, Miss Charity," Sheriff Lillard says. "Seems like a good idea to me. And besides, she's just upset. You need to understand that her property butts right up to your little operation here. I don't blame her for being a little testy."

"Wait, what?" Confusion crowds out the anger for a quick second. "I've never even seen anybody who wasn't a guest. She lives out here?"

Sheriff Lillard nods. "Sure does. Right off mile marker seventy. Been out here a hell of a lot longer than you, so I'd show her some respect."

"Nah," I say. "You don't get to run up on me with a gun and then demand respect. This isn't a game."

He huffs. "Isn't that what you do, Miss Charity? Out here cosplaying the final girl?" His eyebrows lift, and an ugly little smirk creeps across his face. "Mm-hmm," he murmurs. "I've read all about your little operation, and I have to say, I'm not impressed. Don't people have anything better to do?"

Nancy laughs and stares across the parking lot at the lake. "So pretty," she says in a singsong voice. "Be a shame if someone fell in."

Behind me, the crunching of gravel and hurried breaths draw my attention. Bezi and Paige are careening toward me.

"Oh my god! Are you okay?" Bezi asks, grabbing me by the arms and looking me over from head to toe.

"I'm fine. Are you okay?" I turn to Paige. "And you?"

"We're good," Paige says.

I breathe a sigh of relief and pull Bezi close to me.

Sheriff Lillard's face scrunches up, and he turns away. "I'll leave you to it, ladies. I'm going to get Miss Keane some dinner." He looks at his watch. "Maybe breakfast is more appropriate."

Sitting in the back of the car, Nancy is still staring at the nighttime waters of Mirror Lake.

Sheriff Lillard narrows his eyes at me, then tips his hat and climbs into his car, pulling off without another word.

CHAPTER 5

He's gonna take her to eat?" Bezi asks in disbelief. "I mean, I see how people just get away with anything, but damn. Not a citation, nothin'."

"She has to ride in a car with Sheriff Lillard, who I'm just now realizing is a whole asshole," I say. "Maybe that's punishment enough."

Bezi looks absolutely unconvinced but shrugs and slips her hand into mine. "Everybody else left?"

I nod. "It's just us."

"Do I get a raise or something?" Javier asks from the office porch. "None of this shit is in my job description."

"Damn a raise," Porter says. "I'm about to roll out just like everybody else. I do not get paid enough for this. I will call my mama right now."

Tasha steps toward Javier and bats her fake-blood-tinged eyelashes. "You look so cute right now."

Javier looks down at his clothes; fake blood is smeared across his shirt and shorts. He busts out laughing but strides up to Tasha and flicks some of the crusty, dried-up blood off her cheek. "I know. But the question is what are you gonna do about it?"

"Oh my god, please!" Paige says, pinching the bridge of her nose in disbelief. "Are you serious right now? After everything that just happened, y'all flirting?" She shakes her head in disgust. "Immediately no. Y'all cannot do this out here."

"Do what?" Tasha asks.

Paige shoves her hand down on her hip. "Don't do that. Don't act like you don't know the rules."

"Here we go." Bezi chuckles. "Our resident horror-movie scholar."

"Laugh it up," Paige says as she scoots between Tasha and Javier, pushing them away from each other. "As soon as people start having sex, it's like a bat signal to the killer. He hears cheeks clappin', then here he comes with a knife to slice everybody up."

"Paige," I say, my eyes wide. "Nobody is doing that!" Paige is one of those people where it's in her head and out her mouth. I love her, but the secondhand embarrassment is real sometimes.

"Don't speak for me," Tasha says, looking adoringly at Javier, who bites his bottom lip.

Bezi leans close to my ear. "Are the straights okay?"

I have to cover my mouth to keep from laughing. "Absolutely not."

Kyle lets his shoulders round forward and his mouth turn down. "I want to clap some cheeks."

Paige holds the sides of her head like her skull is going to split open. "Have you even watched the movie this place is based on?" Paige is absolutely done with us. "*The Curse of Camp Mirror Lake* is a cautionary tale. It's all right there."

"I've seen it a bunch of times," says Porter. "Doesn't really feel like it's got any super-important life lessons in it. Just people getting filleted left and right."

"I've seen it, like, three or four times," I say.

"I haven't seen it," Bezi says.

Paige turns her head like it's on a swivel. "Well, Bezi, let me enlighten you."

I roll my eyes, and me and Tasha groan in unison. We know how much of a horror stan Paige is, and she is about to break it all the way down for everyone even if nobody really cares.

"How about the short and sweet version?" I suggest. "Nobody wants to hear every single detail."

Paige huffs. "Fine. But ain't shit sweet. It's a pretty messed up movie." She clears her throat and continues. "So *The Curse of Camp Mirror Lake* comes out in 1983. It's a worthy addition to the slasher genre. But it does something the other slasher flicks don't do." She pauses for dramatic effect, and Tasha rolls her eyes so hard, she's gotta be looking at the inside of her own skull.

"Continue," Tasha says. "Damn."

Paige grins. "*The Curse of Camp Mirror Lake* makes it clear that the masked, machete-wielding serial killer Scott Addison gained strength from his victims. Every time he cuts down one of the nine people who die in that movie, he gets stronger, and not just physically."

Porter tilts his head to the side. "He's swinging camp counselors around by their ankles by the time he's three or four bodies in."

"Exactly. And that's what I mean," Paige continues, her voice raising in pitch as excitement takes hold of her. "He's stronger after each kill, but he also starts to do things he couldn't do in the beginning. By midway through the movie, he's faster. He's stealthier. It's almost like he can move without being seen or heard. He gains some kind of supernatural ability as the film goes on, and it's directly related to how many people he kills."

"I remember that," Kyle says. "He always kills them outside too. Like they have to be on the ground or something."

"Right!" Paige says. "Spilling the blood directly on the ground and dumping the bodies in the lake is how the killer gains his power and is able to mow down so many people without anyone knowing until the very end."

"What does any of this have to do with following the horror-movie rules?" I ask.

Paige stares at me like it should be obvious. "People got killed in the movie because they were distracted. Sex, pranks, general recklessness, they're all a distraction. The killer took advantage of the counselors being distracted. You don't get distracted if you want to live."

I put my hand on Paige's shoulder. "I hate to break it to you, but this whole thing"—I gesture to the surrounding woods and cabins—"it's all fake. It's not a movie, Paige. It's just a little fun for people who like to be scared." Something turns in my gut as I say the words. Like, I know they're not entirely true. Images of the figure in the water flood my mind, and I look out over the lake.

Paige crosses her arms hard over her chest. "Whatever. It's all fun and games until you're dead."

"Don't worry," Javier says against Tasha's neck. "I'll protect you."

Tasha smiles way too hard and loops her arm around his waist.

"Well, I'm going to bed," Porter says dramatically, clapping his hands together. "Kyle, you bunking with me tonight, 'cause I'm scared and I'm not afraid to admit that."

Kyle shrugs. "Fine, but you're sleeping next to the door."

"The hell I am," Porter grumbles.

I take Bezi's hand and pull her down the path toward the staff cabins. Kyle and Porter argue about who's going to fight Ms. Nancy Keane if she shows back up and which one of them is going to cover down for Felix if he misses his morning shift again. Tasha and Javier are saying things to each other that no human ears need to hear.

Passing by the lake, I look out over its glassy surface, and a deep sense of foreboding works itself inside my chest and settles there. "I saw something out in the water."

Paige stops dead in her tracks and turns to me. "What?"

"In the lake," I say. I don't want to keep it to myself anymore. I'm bothered by what I saw in a way that I can't shake off. "During the game yesterday. I thought one of the guests went out there and was drowning. I grabbed the life preserver from the lifeguard station and threw it in the water."

"You saw a person?" Bezi asks.

Everyone is looking at me now. "I thought it was—at first. But I kept looking, and they didn't reach for me or try to move. They didn't make a noise or anything." As I think about it, the initial splash was the only noise I'd heard and then nothing but silence. "There was something in the water, but I wasn't sure exactly what." I start to doubt what I saw. Saying it aloud makes it sound ridiculous. A person? Not a person? An animal? I shake my head. "Maybe working out here is getting to me."

Bezi squeezes my hand as she gazes across the lake. "I don't like it."

"It was probably a carp or something," Kyle says. "They're all in the lakes out here and they're huge. They can be three or four feet long. Bigger if they have a food source."

"Maybe," I say, even though I don't believe for one second that what I saw was a fish. This place—in the middle of the woods, far from anything—that's scary enough as it is. It's the setup for almost every slasher film ever. It's *supposed* to be scary. But the truth is that it has never been like that for me—until now. I look away from the water.

"Well, that's enough scary shit for one day," Porter says, ducking inside Staff Cabin #3. "Come on, Kyle."

Kyle rolls his eyes. "If somebody comes in here trying to kill me, I know you're gonna leave me to die."

"Somebody has to be the sacrifice," Porter says.

Kyle shakes his head, looking like every single one of his feelings has been crushed.

Tasha, Paige, and Javier pile into Staff Cabin #1, and I take Bezi into mine.

"Only one bed in here," she says, closing the door and peering past me. "I love that for us."

A smirk creeps its way across my lips. "See, but this isn't a rom-com," I say, slipping my hand around her waist. "It's a horror movie. That means maybe we get to share the bed but there's a hideous monster lurking underneath it, waiting to jump out and get us both."

"Oh, okay," she murmurs, laughing lightly, her hands brushing against the front of my shirt. "You like being out here in the woods, cosplaying the final girl, living your best horror-movie life."

I smile as we let our hands touch, as we let our arms find their way around each other.

"It's better than being home," I say. "That's actually more of a horror-movie environment than this place."

Bezi presses her forehead against mine. "You'd think after

all these years, your mom would see how miserable Rob makes you. He's such a bum."

I sigh. "I'm not the only one who hates him. I low-key think she despises him too. But she won't leave him. She's just—stuck." I shut my eyes. "So that means I have to leave her behind when it comes time."

I want to enjoy my time with Bezi. I don't want to think about home, but that's the thing with Bezi: she makes me feel like I can tell her anything. Like I never have to hold back—good or bad—when I'm with her. The problem is that all this other shit spills out, and that's not what I want right now. I just want her.

Bezi gently caresses the side of my face. "I'm sorry, Charity. You deserve better. You always have."

I open my eyes and stare at her. "I found better—with you. Me and you till the end of the world, right?"

"Maybe even longer than that," she says.

I lean in and press my lips to hers. Soon her hands are under my shirt, pressing against my skin, making me feel warm inside. She suddenly pulls away, and her face scrunches up.

"What?" I ask. "You okay?"

"Yeah, I just— You have fake blood all over you, and your skin is sticky as hell."

I look down at myself, and I'm a complete mess. I have a tendency to forget about anything else in Bezi's presence.

"Sorry," I say. "It's just a little corn syrup." I kiss her again.

"Well, maybe it's not such a big deal," she says against my neck.

I wrap my arms around her, kissing her, running my hands along the slopes and curves of her frame, and then there's a knock at the door. Bezi huffs as I pull away and yank the door open. Paige is standing there, arms crossed, an angry scowl drawing down the corners of her mouth.

"This heffa Tasha booted me out of *our* cabin so that she and Javier can be alone," she says through gritted teeth.

I stick my head out the door to see Tasha staring back at me from the porch of Cabin #1.

"Don't be mad," she yells. "I won't be long."

"The hell?" Javier's voice echoes from inside.

"Whatever," Paige says, turning back to me. "Can I bunk up with you two? I was gonna ask Porter and Kyle, but I don't really know them like that."

I usher her inside and close the door, making sure it's locked.

Bezi kisses me on the cheek. "Later."

"I know I'm messing up y'all's plans," Paige says. "I'm sorry, but I'll be damned if I sleep in a cabin alone tonight."

I squeeze her arm. "You're not messing up anything. Tasha is acting real foolish right now. Not judging, but Javi does not discriminate. He runs through random hookups like serial killers run through camp counselors."

Bezi and Paige both grimace.

I put my hands up. "Like I said, not judging. I don't think either of them is really serious about the other. They're just having fun."

"They put me out like I was supposed to just sleep outside," Paige says. "They having fun and I'm in the woods. That's nice." She rolls her eyes and shoves her hand down on her hip.

"We have a more important issue right now," I say. "We literally only have one bed in here."

Paige's gaze flits to the bed, then back to me. "I'll sleep on the floor. It's not a big deal."

"No," Bezi says. "Nobody's sleeping on the floor. Just curl up at the bottom of the bed. I think we'll all fit." She smiles wide. "It'll be like when we were little. Remember how we used to all sleep on that stank-ass futon in my dad's basement?"

"Oh, man," Paige says. "I'm pretty sure that mutt y'all used to have pissed on that thing."

"Aye," Bezi says, shaking her head. "Don't talk like that about Geneva. She was, like, twenty years old, and she couldn't control her bladder."

"I'm joking," Paige says. "Rest in peace, Geneva!"

"Those were the best sleepovers," I say. "Just endless pizza and soda and scary movies. We should not have been watching *A Nightmare on Elm Street* when we were eight."

"And *Killer Klowns From Outer Space*," Paige says, shaking her head. "That movie is the reason I hate cotton candy to this day."

Bezi laughs. "We thought we were grown. Do y'all remember how we used to go trick-or-treating, then swap costumes and hit up them same houses two or three times?"

"We were a mess," I say, laughing.

"I'm glad we came up," Paige says. "We need to get back to doing stuff like this. I get so busy with the paper. Tasha's working during the school year too." Paige throws a side-ways glance in the direction of Tasha's cabin. "As goofy as she's acting right now, I miss the four of us being together all the time."

"No. I know," I say. "I miss y'all too."

When we're together during the school year, it's nice, but we're all busy with classwork, homework, and babysitting jobs on the weekends. The four of us don't get to hang out as much as we used to, and none of us wants to talk about what that means. Are we growing apart or are we just learning a new way of being friends? I guess we can't eat pizza and watch scary movies forever.

Paige gives me a big hug, then rears back. "Charity, babe. You gotta get this fake blood off you."

Going to the showers this late, and after our little run-in with Ms. Keane, is not happening, so I make use of some baby wipes and a few bottles of water. Bezi shields me with a towel as I wash up as best I can. Paige arranges the pillows and blankets on the bed, and when I'm done, we settle in for the night. Me and Bezi snuggle close to each other while Paige curls up like a cat at the foot of the twin-size bed that definitely is not meant to hold three full-size people. The frame protests—loudly. I just hope it can hang on till morning.

As we lay in the quiet dark, Paige sighs. "You know, if this was a horror movie, Tasha would be sealing our fate by getting it on with Javier. You really think she would do that to us if the stakes were life-and-death?"

Me and Bezi exchange glances, and then all three of us laugh until tears run out of our eyes.

"We'd be doomed," I say through wheezing laughter.

• • •

I'm suddenly lying wide awake, staring up at the ceiling. The cabin is dark aside from the glow of the porch light filtering through the tattered curtains. Bezi is nuzzled up to me. Her rhythmic breaths blow warm and sweet across my neck. At the foot of the bed, Paige is sprawled out, arms and legs spread wide, her foot dangerously close to my face. I nudge her, and she curls into a little ball.

I pull Bezi close to me, and she readjusts herself. In the rustle of clothes and bedsheets, there is a noise. Bezi settles and I hold still, listening. From somewhere outside, in the direction of the lake, there are footsteps. I wonder if maybe Tasha is coming over to apologize to Paige, but I glance at my phone—it's almost three in the morning.

Slipping my arm from under Bezi's head, I roll up and perch myself on the edge of the bed, letting my bare feet rest against the wood floor. The footsteps fade, and after a moment of silence, there is a splash. I'm at the window before I can think, drawing back the curtain just enough to get a look outside. The porch light leaves spots in my vision, and I quickly flip the switch, turning it off.

My eyes adjust to the dark and there, at the far edge of the lake, I think I see something move. I hold my breath and crane my neck, checking to see if the lights are on in any of the other staff cabins. From my vantage point, it's hard to tell. I return my attention to the far side of the lake. There is something, or someone, moving around out there. The figure is hunched over, staggering their steps, pulling something along the ground.

"Bezi," I whisper. "Paige. Get up."

Paige grumbles something to herself as Bezi sits up and readjusts her bonnet.

"What is it?" she asks. "What's wrong?"

"There's somebody out there," I say. There's another loud splash, and I whip my head around, straining to see in the dark.

Bezi stumbles out of bed and joins me at the window. We press our faces close to the glass, fogging it with our breath.

"Where?" Bezi asks.

"Across the lake. Right there." I scan the shoreline until I spot the figure again. This time they're closer to the camp side of the lake, and whatever they were dragging is now gone.

Bezi sighs. "I still don't—"

A hand clamps down on my shoulder, and my heart leaps into my throat as I spin around to find Paige standing directly behind me.

A strangled yelp escapes me. "You almost gave me a heart attack!"

Bezi leans forward and puts her hands on her knees. "Damn, Paige! You just glided over here! No noise or nothing!"

Paige furrows her brow and pulls her bottom lip between her teeth. "You didn't hear me get up?"

"No!" I say.

"Sorry," Paige says. "What's going on?"

I press my hand against my chest like my heart might jump out if I don't. "Look." I pull her toward the window and point to the last place I saw the shadowy figure, only to find nothing but the dark.

"Am I missing something?" Paige asks.

"There was somebody out there," I say. "We saw them."

"Maybe it was Tasha or Porter or somebody else?" Bezi offers. "Should we go check on everybody?" She reaches for the door.

Paige steps in front of her. "Um, no. Text them. We're not going outside at three in the morning because y'all saw some stranger by the lake. Do you know how dumb that sounds?" She shakes her head like she's disappointed in us.

I text Tasha, asking if she's okay. I have to hold my phone over my head to get one funky-ass bar. She responds a few moments later.

TASHA: I'm sleep. So is Javier. Lights are on in P&K's cabin.

I breathe a little easier knowing everyone seems to be all right.

"See?" Paige asks. "Everybody's good, and we didn't even have to go out in the dark and be the first group of people to get horribly murdered."

Bezi waves her off. I nod. She's being overdramatic but I'm glad we didn't go. I can't stop thinking about the stooped figure by the lake. We climb back into bed, and while Bezi and Paige eventually fall asleep, I lie awake listening for the sound of footsteps.

CHAPTER 6

The next morning, I hit the shower, rinsing off the fake blood that has dried in my hair and under my fingernails. I wash my hair, deep condition, then detangle it. I'm sans hair dryer in the summer months, so I pack on a bunch of leave-in and let it air-dry. I feel like a brand-new person as I swap places with Bezi and Paige so they can wash up. Soon as we're all done, I make a beeline to the edge of Mirror Lake.

I lead Bezi and Paige all the way around the east side of the lake. "They were right here," I say, glancing back at the distance to my cabin. "I swear we saw something."

"Maybe it was a bear?" Bezi says.

"No. No way," I say. "It was standing up."

"Bears stand up sometimes," Bezi says.

"You serious?" I ask. "We were looking right at it."

"I didn't have the best view," Bezi says. "And it was dark."

I huff and move closer to the murky water. I peer down into it. I'd heard footsteps and a distinct splash not once but twice. I saw someone. I know I did.

"Check it out," Paige says.

She's wandered a little way from us and is staring down at the ground. I join her and peer at the path that circles the lake. There is a long track in the dirt like something heavy was dragged across its surface. The marks in the dirt stop at the lake's edge.

"You really did see something, didn't you?" Paige asks.

I nod. I know Paige believes me. It goes against all her rules to try and make an excuse for this.

Bezi crouches low to the ground. "You see this?" she asks. She grabs a stick from the nearby brush and pokes around in the dirt, uncovering a wide piece of gnarled gray plastic. On the ends are reinforced holes, and looped through each one is a short length of rusted chain, caked with dirt.

"What is it?" Paige asks. "Trash?"

Bezi shakes her head. "I think it's a swing seat. Like the kind we used to have on the playground in elementary school."

I take the beat-up piece of plastic from her and turn it over in my hands.

"Was there a playground out here?" Bezi asks.

I shake my head. "No. Never. You can't even be up here if you're younger than sixteen." Mr. Lamont had relayed that information to me at some point, but I can't remember the specifics.

A high-pitched clang cuts through the air. I glance across the lake and see Kyle standing on the front steps of the Western Lodge. He's banging a wooden spoon against a pot lid and waving at us.

"Breakfast!" he calls.

I toss the shard of plastic and rusty chains into a trash can as we make our way back to the lodge.

Kyle put together some waffles—the frozen kind—and Porter is setting out orange juice and sliced apples on the big wooden coffee table. Everybody looks as exhausted as I feel. I think I got fifteen minutes of sleep after what we'd seen on the shoreline, and when I woke up with Paige's foot in my back and Bezi's hair in my mouth, I realized that as much as we enjoyed our little sleepover, we're way too grown to be sharing beds.

"Where's Tasha and Javier?" I ask as Bezi falls into the saggy couch and pulls a blanket over herself.

"Probably sleeping in, since they were up late," Porter says. "I don't know what was goin' on over there, but it sounded like two raccoons fighting in a trash can."

Paige gets irritated all over again as she takes up a spot on the love seat across from Bezi. "I can't believe them," she says. "After everything I said. Just callin' out to serial killers." She huffs. "Reckless."

Kyle lowers himself into the love seat next to Paige. "You really believe in stuff like that?"

Paige sighs. "I'm just saying, why chance it? Why do the thing that always leads to somebody getting murdered in the woods?"

I shake my head. "Only in the movies, Paige."

"Whatever," Paige huffs. "After what we saw . . ."

"Wait," Porter says. "What did you see?"

I don't really want to talk about it, so I give him the short and sweet version. "I heard a splash in the lake; then I thought I saw someone on the shoreline."

"Really?" Kyle asks.

I nod.

"I thought I saw somebody out there a few weeks ago," Porter says.

I whip my head around to look at him. "What? Why didn't you say anything?"

He shrugs and waves it off. "People be out in these woods, Charity. Animals too. They weren't there when I checked the next morning. I actually forgot about it until right now. It's nothing."

"I still need to know," I say. "Could have been a trespasser or something."

"I didn't want to bother you, and besides, the season's almost over anyway." Porter gently touches my shoulder. "Listen, I can see that you're tired, and I know you're stressed about the final game and whatever else, but I gotta tell you something."

I sigh. "What is it?"

He points up, and I follow his gesture to the ceiling. Sunlight is slanting through the big rectangular skylight, casting dusty columns of light into the lodge. In the center of the glass is a clearly deceased bird, its neck bent at a weird angle.

"What happened to it?"

"No idea," says Porter. "But we gotta get it down. It's nasty."

"I'll get the ladder," I say. "Just wait here."

Kyle is piling waffles on a plate and Paige is snapping pictures of the big brick fireplace as I leave the lodge and run to the storage shed that's situated right next to the boathouse. The kayaks and canoes bob on the lake as a light breeze ripples the water's surface. The morning light makes the lake look so serene. It's like something off a postcard, but all I can think of when I look at it is the shadowy shape I saw just offshore and the strange figure at the lakeside.

I take the ladder from the shed and drag it back to the lodge, propping it against the side of the building. I grab a stick from the pathway and carry it up. Shimmying onto the roof, I inch myself across to the skylight, where the bird's broken body is splayed out across the glass.

It's an owl.

Its large black eyes are wide open and glassy. They stare into nothingness. Its white-and-gray feathers are ruffled, and its talons are curled into tight knots. It's uncomfortably familiar.

Rob must have had a hundred jobs over the years I've known him, and I think he brought home a little souvenir from every place he'd either quit or been fired from. My room is storage for his collection of failures. Reams of paper from his time at the paper mill sit stacked in the corners. Scrap metal from the recycling center is piled in bins under my window. But the worst thing he ever brought into the house were the taxidermic birds. There were some peregrines and kestrels, other birds of prey, but his favorite were the owls. They lined the shelves in my closet and sat perched on every free inch of space on my dresser. They all have the same dead eyes as the one I'm looking at now.

Staring down into the skylight, I see only my reflection. The glass is meant to see out, not in. I look a mess and quickly move to get the owl off the glass. I prod the owl's lifeless body off the skylight and nudge it down the slope of the roof, where it finally falls over the edge and into the shrubbery below. Disposing of dead animals isn't in my job description, but I do it often. There is always something dying in the woods or in the lake.

I make my way back down the ladder, and Bezi meets me as I hop off the last rung.

"Where is it?" she asks.

"I knocked it into a bush."

Bezi's face twists up. "You just threw it off the side of the roof?"

I interlace my fingers on top of my head and sigh. "I'm sorry? I don't know what else I'm supposed to do."

She stomps off into the bushes and returns a few moments later cradling the dead bird, bits of leaves and grass clinging to her clothes and hair.

"Gross!" Paige says as she steps out onto the porch. "What are you doing?"

Bezi huffs. "You're so insensitive. We can't just leave it in the bushes."

"Babe," I say. "It's—it's dead. Just leave it out there."

Bezi looks at me like I'm insulting her personally. "I want to bury it."

"We're not having a funeral for an owl, Bezi." Paige shoves her hand down on her hip. "You have lost your entire mind. Throw it in the woods and come back inside."

Bezi rolls her eyes and sets the dead bird in the grass just off the pathway.

I put my arms around her, and she leans her head on my shoulder.

"I can't just leave it," she says quietly.

I kiss her cheek and pull her close. "It's okay. I get it."

Bezi wears her heart right on her sleeve. Her mom's a veterinarian and her dad was a park ranger. If it flies, swims, or runs on all fours, she cares about it. She cares about everything and everybody even when she shouldn't, including decomposing owls with broken necks. It's ridiculous, but it happens to be one of the things I love most about her.

"What do you think happened to it?" Porter asks, peering out the door at the bird's crumpled body.

"I don't know," I say. "Its neck was broken. Maybe it flew into the glass."

"It dive-bombed the glass?" Porter asks.

"Does it matter?" Paige asks quietly.

Porter shrugs, and Bezi buries the owl in a shallow grave next to the trail before we retreat back into the lodge.

Kyle brings over a plate of waffles and sets them on the

table. We all settle in and eat and are nearly done when Javier and Tasha come waltzing through the front door. I avoid eye contact. I'm a little annoyed with her, but she falls onto the couch next to me.

"Morning," she says a little too enthusiastically.

"Morning," I say. "Looks like you had a late night."

"You could say that," Tasha says, nudging me in the side. She's got her hair pulled up into a puff on top of her head, and she's wearing Javier's T-shirt.

"It was a rough night for you?" Paige asks sarcastically. "Me, Bezi, and Charity had to share a twin-size bed last night."

Tasha grimaces.

"I'm gonna write a whole piece on this place," Paige says as she makes uncomfortable, unbroken eye contact with Tasha. "About how it brings out the worst in people."

"Like how that one guy with the buzz cut pushed his friend and when he fell stepped on his hand as he was running away?" Tasha asks.

"Yeah," Paige says as she dials up the fake enthusiasm. "And how one of my best friends put me out of the cabin we were supposed to be sharing so she could spend some alone time with some stank-ass boy."

"Hey!" Javier protests.

"Sorry," Paige says. "No offense."

"Uh, full offense taken?" Javier says.

I can't tell if he's mad or just surprised. I bite my lip to keep from smiling, but Porter laughs out loud and doesn't care who hears.

Javier goes to the recliner and sprawls out, shutting his eyes like he's going to sleep. On his right wrist is Tasha's pink hair tie.

"Oh, hell no," I say. "I don't care how late you two were up; we got things to do today, and I need everybody on board because it's just the seven of us."

"Calm down," Javier says dismissively. "I'm here. We're all here. Relax."

"Don't tell her to relax," Paige snaps.

Javier opens his eyes and levels his gaze at her. Paige couldn't care less. She stares right back at him.

"Okay, okay," Porter says, patting the air in front of him. "Let's all take a deep breath. We're all in this together." He turns to me. "I know how much this final game means to you. You're the scream queen of Camp Mirror Lake. But maybe we should call it off. We need more experienced staff, and Felix, Heather, and Jordan decided it wasn't even worth showing up for."

I sigh. "We're booked. A full group. We have to figure it out even if it's just us."

My phone buzzes in my pocket. "Unknown Number" flashes across the screen. I pick it up anyway.

"Hello?"

Static crackles across the line. A voice breaks through in choppy fragments.

". . . signal? Can you . . . hear . . . I can't . . ."

"Who is this?" I ask. I get up and walk around trying to get better reception, but no matter where I am, I can only get one bar.

"Office," the voice says. "Office . . . office phone."

The call drops.

Bezi glances at me. "Who was it?"

"I'm not sure. I think they wanted me to go to the office phone. Everybody stay here." I glance at Tasha and then at Javier. "Especially you two."

Tasha grins, and Javier leans back in the recliner and puts up his feet.

I jog down Path #1, past the boathouse and the campfire site. The lake is murky in the light of day, and I turn away from it as I pass by. I can hear the phone inside the main office ringing before I get inside. I race up the steps and get the door open just as the ringing stops.

I snatch up the receiver, pressing it to my ear. "Hello?"

The sound of the dial tone greets me, and I set the receiver back down. I check my cell phone again. Still only one bar and even that keeps appearing and disappearing. The office phone rings again, and I scramble to grab it before whoever it is hangs up.

"Hello?"

"Charity," a rough voice answers. "You hear me?"

Now that the connection is clear, I know exactly who it is . . . Mr. Lamont.

"Hey, boss," I say.

"Sheriff Lillard called me. Says you were making trouble."

"Excuse me?" A little stab of anger courses through me. "Sheriff Lillard is an asshole. Some woman came up here with a gun and was threatening me and the guests. I wanna know how that makes me the bad guy?"

Mr. Lamont sighs into the phone. "He told me what happened. He and I have never seen eye to eye. I'm not surprised he's blaming you for it."

"Sheriff Lillard says the woman lives close by. I didn't know there was anybody that close—did you?"

"No. And I think I would have noticed if somebody was that close. She's never come around before." There's a long pause. "Charity, listen to me. I need you to shut everything down up there."

"I am," I say. "I invited some friends up to help me because Felix, Jordan, and Heather are no-shows. We'll have everything locked up and shut down in a few days."

"No," he says gruffly. "I mean right now. No final game tonight, Charity. Shut it down until I figure out how to handle this."

"What?" My heart sinks. I really want my shot at being the final girl in the last game. I've been looking forward to it all season. "What do you mean? We're shutting it down because some crazy old lady showed up here?"

Mr. Lamont grumbles something unintelligible into the phone before continuing. "The sheriff is not so subtly hinting that I could be sued."

"For what?" I ask, anger bubbling up. "We have waivers in place so people can't sue us."

"This woman wasn't a guest," Mr. Lamont says. "I don't know if I believe what Sheriff Lillard is saying, but he's made it clear that he doesn't mind making things difficult for us. I don't know what his angle is, but I can't afford a lawsuit and I need to figure out how I'm going to handle this. Shut it down. Call me when it's done. And Charity . . ." He trails off.

"Yeah?" I ask, trying hard not to let the disappointment show in my voice.

"That woman who came up there, what did she say to you?"

I slump down on the stool behind the desk. "She was just yelling and waving that gun around. She made it sound like this was her property and that she knew something about it that we don't. She said, 'If you knew what I know.' What does that even mean?"

Mr. Lamont's heavy sigh pushes through the phone. "I don't know, but this is absolutely ridiculous. It's always something." There's a pause. "Listen, I know how much you look forward to the final games. They're always the highlight of our season, but this is serious. Go ahead and close it down, refund the guests. Try not to be too upset. Give me some time to sort this out. We'll be back on track next season. Don't you even worry about it."

The phone clicks, and the line goes dead. I stare at the receiver in my hand for a solid ten seconds before I hang up.

I grab the guest register and call the people who'd made

their reservation for that night. They're pissed and they attempt to take it out on me, cussing at me, telling me I ruined their plans. I politely tell them that their deposit will be refunded, then hang up. I'm not in a customer's-always-right kind of mood. I trudge back to the Western Lodge and sit next to Bezi.

"What's wrong?" she asks.

I look around. Javier looks like he's actually asleep, and as Paige follows my gaze, she promptly gets up and kicks the side of the recliner. Javier bolts awake, confused.

"Listen," I say. "That was Mr. Lamont on the phone. He says the final game is canceled."

"What?" Kyle asks. "Are you serious?"

"Yeah," I say. "I already called the guests and let them know not to come up. I guess Sheriff Lillard called Mr. Lamont and told him we were the ones making trouble with that lady."

"Ummm," Porter says. "She's the one who brought a gun up here!" He stands and angrily crosses his arms over his chest. "Sheriff Lillard took that chick to get breakfast. He wasn't concerned, so why would he call Mr. Lamont at all?"

"I don't know," I say. "But it doesn't even matter. Mr. Lamont wants it shut down." I sigh and lean back on the couch. "We can move our stuff in here. That way we can shut down all the other buildings. Save kitchen for last. It shouldn't take us that long if we all pitch in."

Bezi interlaces her fingers with mine and squeezes my hand. "I'm sorry. I know you were looking forward to the final game."

I always look forward to the last game, but closing down a

day early means I'll have to head home a day early, and that's the last thing I want.

"It's okay," Tasha chimes in. "It'll be like a big sleepover. It'll be fun."

"You gonna kick us out of here, too, so you and Javier can have the place to yourselves?" Paige asks.

Tasha bum-rushes Paige and wraps her up in a bear hug. "Don't be mad at me. I love you, and if you be nice to me, I'll let you tell me some scary stories in front of the fireplace."

Paige tries to act like she's still mad but gives up almost immediately. Her and Tasha are like sisters. They can't stay mad at each other for too long, and Paige can never pass up an opportunity to share her encyclopedic knowledge of scary stories.

"I'm gonna tell you a story that'll make you want to sleep with one eye open," Paige says. "And it's about this place."

I glance at her. "What do you mean?"

Paige presses her lips together. "Let's just say I did a little digging before I came up here, and there are some really messed up stories about Mirror Lake."

Tasha lays her head on Paige's shoulder. "Sounds like a plan. Just as long as you're not mad at me anymore. Honestly, I should have booted him, not you." She rolls her eyes, but Javier is too busy trying to go back to sleep to notice. Tasha waltzes over to him and snatches her hair tie off his wrist and slides it onto her own.

"I think we can shut down all the staff and guest cabins

today," I say. "We'll leave the showers, kitchen, and main lodge for tomorrow. Then all that'll be left is locking everything up and closing the office and control center. Everybody pitches in. We get it done and get home. Deal?"

"Deal," says Kyle. "I'm ready to get up outta here."

"Same," says Porter. "Let's go."

CHAPTER 7

We spend the morning cleaning cabins—stripping the sheets and blankets and stuffing them into watertight storage bags, making sure all the windows are closed and locked. When I shut off the main breaker, the electricity to the whole place will go out, so that gets saved for last. Me and Bezi drag canoes out of the lake and stack them against the side of the boathouse. I can't help but think about what I saw by the lakeside, but the sooner we get everything done the sooner we can leave. Porter helps Kyle take out the trash; Tasha and Paige cover the firepit and sweep out the stripped-down cabins. Javier helps us bring all our personal belongings into the Western Lodge.

I'm helping Bezi sweep out the storage shed when Javier waltzes past with an armful of blankets and pillows.

"What about the big cabin?" he asks.

I tilt my head back and let a long breath hiss out from between my lips. "I completely forgot about that," I say.

"We gotta strip down another staff cabin?" Bezi asks.

"Jordan, Heather, and Felix were bunking together in one of the bigger cabins on the west side of camp. I completely forgot."

Bezi huffs. "We can probably knock it out if we head over there now."

I nod, and we make our way to the guest cabins that are situated down a steep slope behind the main office. The cabins in this part of camp sleep eight, and we only use them once or twice a season when big groups come to play the game.

Bezi and I cut through the thick grass and climb the steps of Cabin #6. The curtains in the front window are partway open, and I try to peer inside, but the screen is thick with dirt and dead bugs. I try the door, but it's locked.

"You have a key?" Bezi asks.

"Don't really need one," I say. "It's a twist lock." I turn the handle hard to the right and shoulder check the door. It pops open.

The smell knocks me back immediately. I quickly cover my nose and mouth with my hand, and Bezi gags.

"Oh my god, what is that smell?" she asks, her eyes watery.

I pull my shirt up over my nose and scan the room. Sitting on the wooden table in the center of the room is a plate of food. Chicken breast, broccoli, and rice. I try to remember when we had that meal. I remember the broccoli tasting like garbage so

I dumped mine. It had to have been this past Thursday, which also happened to be the last time all the staff were on shift and accounted for. The food is rotted and crawling with gnats and flies. I stifle the urge to vomit as I grab a trash can and sweep the food—plate and all—into the can and set it outside the front door.

"They just left that here?" Bezi asks. "Rude."

Jordan and Heather had been no-shows on Friday, and Felix hadn't shown up for his shift either. The three of them had come to work at Mirror Lake together; Heather took her job seriously, but Jordan and Felix treated it like this was their own personal summer camp. They were chronically late and their acting skills were questionable, which pissed me off because the whole point of this place is to convince the guests that they're in real danger.

Besides the spoiled food and dirty dishes, they've left their dirty clothes in a basket by the window, the beds are unmade, and Jordan's phone is sitting on the bedside table. The screen is cracked, and when I tap the broken glass, it doesn't even light up.

"It's dead," I say.

"She just left her phone?" Bezi asks. "And they left their clothes?"

"They must have left in a rush, but I didn't even see them leave and they didn't say anything to me about going home early." None of them had a car, so somebody must have come up to get them.

"Some people are just inconsiderate," Bezi says as she yanks the covers off Felix's bed and balls them up.

I set Jordan's phone back down and take out my own. The staff group chat message to Jordan, Felix, and Heather is still unsent. I try sending it again, and this time it goes through.

By the time Bezi and I are done cleaning, it's almost three in the afternoon, and we head back to the Western Lodge, exhausted. When we get there, everyone else is already settled inside.

"How'd it go?" Kyle asks.

"Jordan, Heather, and Felix left a mess in their cabin," I say. "There was stuff everywhere and Jordan left her phone."

Porter sucks his teeth. "They hated it here that much?"

I shrug. "It's weird. There were dirty clothes in there and a plate of rotten food on the table."

Javier scrunches up his nose. "Nasty."

"Do you think we'll be able to get out of here by tomorrow?" Kyle asks.

"I think so," I say. "I'm over it. I just want to eat and curl up on the couch."

"I got hot dogs going," Kyle says. "I think we're out of chips, though."

Porter hops up and makes a beeline back to the staff lockers in the Western Lodge's back room. He emerges a few moments later with two party-size bags of chips. "Felix thought he was slick. I saw him hide these in his locker last week, and since he left us to pick up the slack, it's only fair we get to raid his stash."

Porter portions out the chips, and we all devour our food like we haven't eaten in days. Javier lies across his pile of blankets in front of the big fireplace, and me and Bezi get comfy on the couch. Kyle sits in the recliner and scarfs down at least four hot dogs while Paige and Tasha try to decide on what scary story Paige is going to tell when it gets dark. I may not be playing the final girl tonight, but at least I get to have some fun anyway.

"There's one about the guy who breaks in and the kid who's home alone hides in the dryer," Paige offers. "You can probably guess how that one turns out."

"I've heard that one and it's awful," Tasha says.

Kyle leans forward. "What about that one—what's it called?—thump, drag?"

"Thump, thump, drag," Paige corrects. "And that's more of an urban legend, but I could tell it if you want."

"Sounds boring," Javier says.

Paige rolls her eyes. "You got any suggestions?"

Javier shrugs like he couldn't care less what story she tells.

"You said you were gonna tell us something about the lake," I say. "Why don't you save the real scary stuff for later and tell us about the lake now."

Tasha tilts her head to the side. "Wait. What about the lake?"

Paige rubs her hands together and smiles. "Okay. So if you google this place, the only thing that really comes is all the stuff about the filming of *The Curse of Camp Mirror Lake* and about what you do here now with the terror simulation. But at the town archives, they have stuff on microfilm that's not even on the Internet."

"Microfilm?" Kyle asks.

"It's like old-school PowerPoint. Pictures of other pictures and documents all put together on a reel."

Kyle looks like his brain is about to implode, but he doesn't ask any more questions.

"And how is it not on the Internet?" Porter asks. "Everything is on the Internet."

"Not this," Paige says. "There was an actual summer camp here back in the day."

I glance at Paige, expecting her to laugh and tell me she's joking, but she doesn't.

"What?" she asks. "Why are you looking at me like that?"

I lean forward and rest my elbows on my knees. "Paige, no. There's never been an actual camp out here. I think there was an RV park on the other side of the lake at some point but that's it."

"If there was a camp here, somebody would have known," says Tasha. "With the movie being filmed here, something like that would be public knowledge."

Paige shakes her head. "No. I saw pictures and everything. The stuff in the Groton archives hasn't been digitized at all. Ms. Grandey, the woman who organizes all the stuff there, is, like, a hundred years old. I go in there all the time for the school paper, so I know what they have, but this stuff about the summer camp—nobody would know unless they were specifically looking for it."

I sit back and try to take in what Paige is saying. My gaze drifts to the window, to the lake, where only a little while ago I found the remnants of a swing set. I'm not sure that that means a summer camp existed on these grounds, but I want to know more.

"What did you find?" I ask.

Paige takes out her phone and reads from some notes she took. "It wasn't much. Most of the mentions of it were in newspapers. I found one from 1960 and one from 1961. The first one was talking about a grand opening, but it's so blurry, I could hardly make it out. The second one was talking about the lake. There was a picture. Look."

She turns her phone toward me, and I stare at the faded contrasts in the overexposed picture. There's a body of water and lifeguard tower, but it's impossible to tell if it's actually Mirror Lake or not.

"It was private," Paige says. "The clipping made it sound like only rich folks could bring their kids up to the camp."

Porter crosses and uncrosses his legs like he can't get comfortable. He avoids my eyes as I shift my gaze to him.

"Porter?" I ask. "Something you want to share?"

He purses his lips and then sighs. "In my defense, I thought it was a prop left over from when they shot the movie, so I didn't bring it up."

A little ripple of unease pulses through me. "What are you talking about?"

Porter sighs and clasps his hands together in front of him. "I was doing a walk-through when I first got hired, just tryna get a good handle on the layout of the camp, and I found something out there behind the supply shed." He leans forward. "There was this mound of dirt. It looked out of place, so I went to check it out." He pinches the bridge of his nose. "It was all overgrown, but on the back side there was wood sticking out. Like an upside-down canoe. The letters on the side said 'Camp Mirror Lake.'"

I exhale in frustration. "You didn't think I should know about that?"

Porter shrugs. "Like I said, I thought it was a prop. Maybe it is. I don't know."

"Okay, well, so what?" Kyle asks. "Why do we care if it was a summer camp?"

He's right, I guess. I guess it doesn't matter, but it doesn't sit right with me. Did Mr. Lamont know? And if so, why hide it?

"What did that lady with the shotgun say?" Bezi suddenly asks. She thinks for a minute. "If we knew what she knows? Do you think this camp has something to do with what she was saying?"

"Wish we knew for sure that it even existed," Tasha says.

Paige huffs and slumps down in her seat. "It did."

"We could ask my grandma," Javier offers.

We all turn to look at him.

"Why?" Kyle asks.

"She was born in Groton," he says. "And she's nosy. She's always in everybody's business, especially the old ladies she plays cards with on Saturdays." Javier readjusts himself on the blankets. "My grandma's . . . protective. I'm her favorite grand-kid. She has, like, twenty. So it's a big deal."

Kyle bats his eyes dramatically. "Oh, that's so cute. You're Grandma's favorite?"

"Shut up," Javier says. "The point is that there was no way she was gonna let me work at a horror-simulation camp. So I made some shit up so she wouldn't worry. Told her it was a summer camp. When I told her it was up here in the woods, she started acting weird."

"Weird?" Kyle asks. "What's that mean?"

"She was asking me not to go," Javier says. "Then she was *telling* me not to go. She said I wasn't allowed to take the job but bills gotta get paid and she's only getting her social security check. I couldn't really say no to it."

I give Javier a tight smile. He's always so busy acting like he's god's gift, it's easy to forget he's got a life outside of this place, problems at home just like everybody else.

"Call her," I say. "How many bars you got?"

"One," he says. "Signal is terrible, but I'll try."

He dials the number. The call drops and he tries again. It goes through the second time, and he puts the phone on speaker.

"Hello?" A voice crackles across the line.

"Grandma," Javier says. "I have a question for you."

She sighs. "You just call me and ask questions. Don't even say how are you?"

Javier grimaces. "Sorry. How are you?"

Tasha smiles, and even Kyle softens a little at the exchange.

"Terrible!" Javier's grandma says dramatically. "You're gone for so long. I don't like it. When are you coming home?"

"A couple more days," Javier says. "But I have a question."

"What is it?" she asks.

"I know you didn't really want me to come up to the camp for the summer."

"That's not a question," she grumbles.

"No, I know," he says quietly. "I wanted to ask if you know anything about a summer camp that was here at some point? Maybe it was a long time ago. We're not sure."

There is a long silence, and it is filled with a terrible sinking feeling. I shift uncomfortably in my seat and lean toward the phone.

"Why are you asking me this?" Javier's grandma asks. Her tone is dark, her breaths coming in long, slow draws over the static on the line.

Javier glances at me, and I silently urge him to press her about it.

"When I told you I was coming up here, you didn't want me to," says Javier. "Why? Does it have anything to do with the camp that was here before?"

There is another pause, and then her voice crackles through the phone again. "It was 1971, but yes. There was a camp."

I inhale sharply, and Paige gives me her best I-told-you-so glare.

"I have some friends here," Javier says. "We work together. Nobody knows about the camp that was here before. We don't understand why nobody told us."

"I don't want to talk about it," she says. His grandmother's tone sends a chill up my back. She sounds angry, but there's something else in her voice, something that makes me hold my breath as she prepares to answer.

"I want you to leave. I never should have let you go." She begins to mumble. It sounds almost like a prayer. "Leave. You have a ride? I'll come get you."

"You don't drive," Javier says. "You haven't driven a car since before I was born. You don't even have a license."

I suddenly feel like I'm intruding on a private conversation.

"I don't care," Javier's grandma says.

"I shouldn't have brought it up," Javier says. "We need the money. You can't handle the bills all by yourself and—"

"People died up there!" Javier's grandma says suddenly. "Six kids your age. Dead! In one night."

My heart somersaults in my chest. Where only a minute ago the room was filled with the awkwardness of listening to Javier have a disagreement with his grandmother, there's now a void that is slowly being filled by an overwhelming dread.

"What—what is she talking about?" I ask, still feeling like I can't move or breathe.

Tasha scoots in and puts her mouth close to the phone. "When? When was this?"

"The summer I worked there, six people got killed, but they never found—" Static chokes her words. "I—no one knew— survivor—leave now! Leave!" The call drops and the line goes silent.

CHAPTER 8

I stare at Javier. "Get her back on the phone."

Javier fumbles with his phone, redials his grandma's number, but can't get through.

"It's the signal," he says. He stands up and walks around the lodge, holding his phone out like that'll make a difference.

"Holy shit," Tasha says. "There was a camp here and people actually died?"

"No way," Paige whispers. "There was nothing in the archives about anybody dying. Not from what I saw."

"What the hell is going on?" Kyle asks. "I thought the only thing that happened was that they made that slasher flick. That's why people come up here, right?"

I struggle to put it all together. As far as I know, the thing that makes Camp Mirror Lake special is that they filmed a cult classic here, but if what Javier's grandmother said is true, we're on the site of a mass murder.

"How do we not know about this?" I ask. "How is that possible?"

"Maybe she's lying?" Porter suggests.

Javier turns and marches back to where we're all gathered. "You calling my grandma a liar?"

Porter puts his hands up in front of him. "Bad choice of words. Sorry. I just mean, maybe she's misremembering. How old is she anyway?"

"Seventy next month," Javier says without missing a beat. "And she's not misremembering anything. If she says that's what happened, that's it. Take her word for it."

"Okay, okay," Porter says. "I believe her, okay?"

Javier tries to get her back on the phone with no luck.

I sit quietly for a moment. "You think your grandma knows Ms. Keane?"

"Who?" Javier asks.

"The shotgun lady," I say. "When she was here, she said, 'If you knew what I know.' Do you think she knows what happened here? She kept asking if this was all just a game to us. It sounded like she thinks what we're doing here is disrespectful. Maybe she's not talking about the movie at all."

"I mean, it literally is a game for us," Porter says.

"That has to be what she meant when she said we should be ashamed of what we're doing here," I say. "We're really out here just walking over the place where a bunch of people died?"

"There's always someone who has a piece of the untold story," Paige says quietly. "That's part of the rules of horror too."

"Not now, Paige. Damn," Tasha says.

"Didn't that sheriff guy say Ms. Keane lived close by?" Paige asks as she types furiously on her phone. "I'm making notes of everything, but he did say that, didn't he?"

I shrug. "Yeah. So?"

"So don't you think we should know if we're walking over people's bones and shit?" Paige stands up. "I'm a reporter. This is huge. We gotta go talk to her and find out what she knows." She turns to Javier. "I need to talk to your grandma at some point, but right now we gotta go see this Keane lady."

"Wait a minute," Tasha says. "Paige, I know you take your job at the school seriously, but—"

"Very seriously," Paige cuts in. "I'm going to college for journalism. You know this. Imagine what this will look like on my résumé. I help uncover Camp Mirror Lake's shady past?" She squeals. "Get up. We're going."

"You don't even know how to get there," Porter says.

"But you do," Paige says. "Charity is always saying that you know this place like the back of your hand. I bet you know where the property line is and all the trails, huh? You telling me you've never once hopped the fence and gone exploring?"

The corners of Porter's mouth lift into a little smirk that tells me he has definitely done exactly that.

"The woods are not the place to be playing around," I say.

"It's not like a city park out there. It's a forest. It's hundreds of acres. There are bears and who knows what else."

"People still use the trails," Porter says. "Some of them are pretty worn. It's trespassing on whoever owns the land behind Camp Mirror Lake, but that doesn't stop them."

"Right," I say. "But I think we're forgetting the most important thing." Everybody is looking at me like I have two heads. "Ms. Keane came up here with a shotgun. She didn't even get in trouble. Now y'all wanna go try to interview her? She'll probably shoot you as soon as she sees you."

Paige is already gathering her stuff and slipping on her shoes.

Bezi stands up and crosses her arms hard over her chest. "You are not going."

"Oh, I'm going," Paige says. "Come on, Porter. You can't pass up the opportunity to show off your trail navigation skills."

I glance at Porter. Paige is right. He's already pulling on his shoes. He's such an important part of our team because he knows his way around these woods, but even he can't know what's too far beyond the fence surrounding the camp.

"This is ridiculous," I say.

"Route 710 is southeast of the trail that runs from the supply shed," Porter says. "And Sheriff Lillard said she was at mile marker seventy, right? We're right off mile marker sixty-eight, so she's less than two miles from here at the most."

"This all feels really, really stupid," Kyle chimes in. "You're gonna just knock on her door?"

"The sheriff didn't seem too concerned about her," Tasha says. "Maybe she's just a little . . . off."

I look at her like she's lost her mind. "You're siding with them?"

Paige marches up to me and takes me by the shoulders. "Listen, if we go now, we'll be back before it gets dark. I'll have my story and maybe I can mend fences so she won't come up here anymore. Porter knows the way." She turns to Tasha. "You coming? You owe me anyway."

Tasha hesitates. "I mean—yeah, I guess."

Bezi sucks her teeth. "This is so stupid. Isn't this against the rules, Paige? Isn't there some horror movie theme about not marching off into the woods to investigate some weird shit you heard or saw?"

"At night," Paige says. "Only at night when it's dark. *That* would be against the rules."

Bezi throws her hands up in defeat and slumps down into the couch. Tasha comes over and puts her hand on my shoulder.

"It's three," she says. "We'll be back by six." She squeezes my arm and leads a determined Paige and a way-too-giddy Porter out the front door.

"Well, I guess we're never gonna see them again," Javier says.

"Shut up, Javi," Kyle says. "It's not funny."

The sun slants through the big picture windows at the front of the lodge, and dust swirls in the shifting columns of light. I sit next to Bezi and try to think in a straight line.

"According to Javier's grandma, there was a summer camp here in 1971. That's twelve years before they shot *The Curse of Camp Mirror Lake*. And she's saying six people died, but I've never heard of anything like that."

"I hate to be morbid, but you'd think if something like that really happened here, it might get mentioned more," Bezi says. "I feel like it'd be a selling point for this place."

Kyle looks appalled. "Jesus."

"I'm not saying I agree," Bezi says quickly. "I'm just sayin'." She sits up straight.

"What?" I ask. "What is it?"

"I forgot—I meant to tell you." She shakes her head. "When Ms. Keane was waving her gun around, me and Paige barricaded the door in the control center, but we still didn't feel safe so we, uh—we kicked in that locked supply closet."

"What?" I ask. "Did you damage anything?"

Bezi purses her lips.

"Bezi, come on." I sigh. "I gotta fix it if you broke something. There's expensive equipment in there."

"No there isn't," she says. "That's what I'm saying. There's no equipment in there at all. Just boxes of junk. Mostly papers and folders from what we could see."

I pause. "Mr. Lamont said it was extra audio and video equipment. He said it was more valuable than anything else we have out here."

Bezi shrugs. "Maybe there's something in there that your boss doesn't want y'all to see."

I stand and pull Bezi up with me. "Come on. I want to go have a look." I turn to Javier and Kyle. "Y'all coming?"

"Nah," Javier says. "I'm tired. I'm gonna take a nap until Tasha and them come back."

"I need to start cleaning out the kitchen," Kyle says. "We're still tryna get out of here tomorrow, right?"

"Yeah," I say. "As long as we get everything done. Day after tomorrow at the latest."

Kyle looks severely disappointed.

"I'll be back to help in a little bit," I say.

He gives me a smile, and Bezi and I head to the control center.

• • •

The door to the supply closet in the control room is halfway off the hinges and the frame is cracked around the lock plate. I narrow my eyes at Bezi. "Y'all busted this thing wide open."

"We were scared," Bezi says. "My adrenaline was pumping. Sorry. I think we can fix it, though."

I nudge the broken door open and glance inside the large closet. Bezi is right; there's no extra equipment, just dozens of boxes filled with file folders and paper. A thick, musty odor lingers in the air and there's a layer of gray dust on everything. A skitter of tiny feet tells me some mice have made this place their home. I grab one of the boxes nearest me and open its water-damaged flaps. Inside are a few folded shirts and red whistles on strings. I pull out one of the tops and hold it up. It's filled with holes where mice or moths or some other creature ate their way through the fabric. Across the front of the yellow shirt in big red letters that have faded so much they're nearly invisible, I can just make out the words CAMP MIRROR LAKE and underneath that, the word COUNSELOR.

"These are uniforms?" Bezi asks. "Like from the movie?"

I try to think about the details of *The Curse of Camp Mirror Lake*. "No," I say after racking my brain. "In the movie, the shirts were white, and the lettering was black."

Bezi opens another box and finds a stack of moldering paper. She quickly closes the lid and pulls her shirt up over her nose and mouth.

"Gross," she says. "There's mold all over it. I don't wanna breathe this stuff in. Who knows how long it's been sitting back here."

"Years, from the looks of it," I say. It's weird that Mr. Lamont lied about what was in the closet. There doesn't seem to be anything in here warranting a padlock and a whole-ass cover story.

I push around some more boxes and find another one filled to bursting with yellowing newspaper clippings, their edges winnowed by some kind of insect that has an appetite for old newsprint. I know because the bugs ate their fill and left behind their translucent corpses when they died. I dust the bodies away and thumb through the first few pages to find several articles about campers missing after a bear was sighted in the area around Mirror Lake. The dates on the papers are from 1976 to

1978. I dig through and find another article dated October 1983, panning the release of *The Curse of Camp Mirror Lake* and saying the only people who are drawn to horror films are deviants and weirdos. I make a mental note not to share this little critique with Paige when she gets back.

Closer to the bottom of the stack is a tan folder. I pull it out and dump the contents onto the lid of another box so I can look through. A clipping from the *Groton Tribune* reads, *Summer camp closes. Disappearances attributed to inexperienced campers and camp staff.*

"Bezi, look at this."

Bezi peers over my shoulder. "It says *summer camp.* It's gotta be what Javier's grandma was talking about, right? I guess she was telling the truth after all."

"The camp existed, but it doesn't say anything about campers being killed." I set the papers down. "Why does Mr. Lamont have this stuff?"

"When did he buy this place?" Bezi asks. "Maybe he just hasn't gone through all this junk."

"Why would he tell me it's expensive supplies and not to mess with it, then?" I ask. "He's trying to hide what happened here? Why? It makes no sense." I dig through more scraps and don't find anything else about the camp, but I do find several articles about the purchase of the land itself under a nest of silverfish. I shake off the silvery bugs, some of which are still squirming, to find attached to the paper a photocopy of a deed. I gently smooth it out. Dead center is an approximation of

Mirror Lake. South of the water is a highlighted area labeled *proposed site of summer camp*, but the lines and measurements indicating the perimeters of the camp extend far beyond the fenced area.

"I wish Porter was here," I say. "He could tell me what this all means. To me, it looks like at some point somebody bought up this site and all the land behind it. But this is from the sixties. Mr. Lamont isn't that old, I don't think."

"Weird," Bezi says as she stares down at the deed. "Let's take it back to the lodge and show Kyle and Javier, see what they think."

I gather up the clippings and the copy of the deed and stick them back in the tan envelope. Bezi and I are on our way out when something catches my attention on one of the monitors in the control center. I stop and lean closer to the screen.

"What is it?" Bezi asks.

"The camera that monitors the trapdoor under the boathouse is out," I say as I stare at the blank screen.

"Why?" Bezi asks.

"Not sure," I say. All the other monitors are on and showing their designated areas in black and white. "The cameras are pretty new, but I gotta check it before we shut everything down so Mr. Lamont knows to fix it before next season. If there even is a next season."

Bezi loops her arm under mine and pulls me toward the door.

"It'll be fine," she says reassuringly.

I lean against her shoulder, wanting so much to believe her when suddenly, for just a split second, the broken camera blinks on and I see a figure, cloaked in black, standing just under the hatch that leads up through the floor of the boathouse.

CHAPTER 9

The camera blinks off again, and the screen goes dark.

"Did you see that?" I ask.

Bezi glances back at me. "What?"

"I saw someone in the tunnel under the boathouse hatch."

"Who?" Bezi asks. "Kyle or Javier?"

"I—I couldn't tell." The lighting down there is low on purpose. We don't want the guests knowing we have access to trapdoors and secret tunnels. It adds to the illusion of the game, but nobody is supposed to be down there now that the final game is canceled. The camera flickers back on, and whoever was standing there is now gone.

"Come on," I say.

We leave the control center and walk along the edge of Mirror Lake as a cool breeze whips the surface into a cascade of ripples. The water is muddy, dark, and almost impossible to see through as it laps against the sandy shoreline.

"I wish we could have gotten more information out of Javier's grandma. She sounded really upset that he was up here."

"She was willing to drive up to get him and she doesn't even have a license," Bezi says.

I hold the envelope of clippings tight. "Like, what happened? Maybe the people running the camp were reckless or something? You can't have people up here and just turn them loose. Hikers and campers get lost in the woods all the time. People drown in lakes and rivers. There are wild animals. It's dangerous."

"Maybe," says Bezi, sighing. "It's not like people had seen something like *Friday the 13th* or *The Curse of Camp Mirror Lake* back then. Paige is always talking about the rules of horror, but she gets all that from watching movies. People like Javier's grandma didn't have references like that."

"I guess," I say as we approach the Western Lodge. "I still don't like the fact that Mr. Lamont was lying to me about what was in that closet."

We're crossing the dirt trail that runs in front of the lodge when Bezi tightens her grip on my arm. Her face is a mask of confusion, and as I follow her gaze, I see why. The little mound of dirt where she buried the dead owl is turned up. The dark, damp soil is scattered across the grass and on the trail. Bezi lets go of my arm and takes a step toward the little grave, but I grab hold of her.

"No," I say, my heart thudding in my chest. "Wait here. I'll check."

She stands in silence as I approach the hole in the ground.

"Well?" Bezi asks, not bothering to lift her gaze from the ground immediately in front of her.

"It's—it's empty." My throat suddenly feels tight, like I can't breathe. I pull at the collar of my shirt. "Sometimes animals do this," I say, trying to think if that's a real thing that happens. "They could probably smell it."

Bezi presses her lips together and shakes her head. I quickly gather her up and lead her to the lodge, but we only make it to the second step when we learn the terrible fate of the deceased owl. Bezi gasps, but I can't breathe at all. The owl's broken body lies on the welcome mat of the lodge, just outside the front door. Dirt clings to its feathers, and it's intact except for the eyes—those blank, glassy eyes that were so much like Rob's hideous collection of dead things—that have been plucked out of its head.

Bezi screams, and the sound cuts through my brain like a knife. Footsteps sound from inside, and a moment later, Javier flings open the door. He looks like he just woke up, and Kyle is right behind him carrying two black trash bags. They immediately register the dead bird.

"What the hell is this?" Javier asks, crouching down to get a better look.

"Another owl?" Kyle asks.

I rush Bezi inside, and both Javier and Kyle come in behind us. I steer Bezi to the couch and make her sit.

"Not a different owl," I say. "The same one. Something dug it up."

Javier and Kyle exchange confused glances.

"How is it the same one?" Javier asks. "Bezi buried it."

"I don't know, Javi!" I shout. "Just give me a minute to think!"

Silence swallows the room. My mind goes in circles as I try to justify the reappearance of the decomposing owl.

"Something, some animal, must have dug it up and dragged it onto the porch," I say once I've gathered myself enough to do more than just yell at Javier.

"What animal?" Kyle asks quietly. "I can't think of anything that would do that."

"Dogs would," I say. "Dogs can do that."

Kyle presses his lips together. "When have you ever seen a dog out here, Charity? And it was on the porch. If an animal dug it up, wouldn't it take it somewhere and eat it?"

Bezi groans, and I gently rub her back. Kyle's right, but I don't know what that means. *Something* dug up that owl and put it on the mat.

"I don't wanna talk about it anymore," Bezi says. "We have to do something with it, though."

"I'll take care of it," Kyle says. He disappears out the door, trash bags in hand, and returns a few minutes later. He gives me a nod. "Did you guys find anything in the control center?" he asks.

I'm happy to change the subject, and I can tell by the way Bezi sighs that she is too.

"Maybe," I say, setting the envelope of newspaper clippings on one of the tables in front of the couch. "That room Mr. Lamont told me was storage for extra equipment is just a room full of moldy old boxes. We found a bunch of stuff, but I wanted to show you these." I spread the clippings out across the table. "This article is from 1962, and it says a camper went missing from this exact area and that their remains were never recovered. There're a few more just like this from '62 to '71. And then this from late 1971. It's a little blip in a local paper, but it says the summer camp that was right here on these grounds closed. It doesn't say what happened."

"My grandma told you what happened," Javier says. "Six kids dead in one night. You think she's lying?"

"I didn't say that," I say firmly. "I don't know what to think. If six people were massacred in the woods, there would be more about it, right? A lot of people don't really like what we do here. They're always looking for ways to try and get this place shut down, but it never happens. Somebody would have dragged this up at some point, right? They'd be shouting about it to make us seem like insensitive jerks."

Bezi nods. "Paige said she has access to all kinds of archives and stuff, but are they just things about Groton? Maybe she can try another town close by to see if it got reported there—Cortland or Ithaca, maybe?"

"And we don't think Mr. Lamont knows about this?" Kyle asks. "Or what—he's covering it up?"

"I mean, he specifically told me not to go in that storage room," I say. "And he lied about what was in there, so I think he knows *something*."

"It could go either way," Javier says. "Mr. Lamont might like the fact that some kids got killed up here and is just waiting for the right way to market it, or he might think it's terrible and just not want anyone to know what happened."

I guess it could be either of those things, but I don't know Mr. Lamont well enough to decide which is more likely. I've only been in the same room with him a handful of times, and mostly we just talk on the phone. I really hope he isn't planning on using the deaths as some kind of marketing tool. That just doesn't sit right with me. I pick up my phone to call Mr. Lamont, but I don't have a signal.

"Great," I mumble. I glance at the time. It's pushing five o'clock. "I wish Tasha and them would hurry up and get back. It's gonna get dark soon."

"Paige thinks she's some investigative journalist or something," Bezi says. "And Tasha's just going right along with it."

I nudge Bezi with my shoulder. "You know how they are. It's always all or nothing with them."

Bezi nods and rests her head on my shoulder.

"I can make dinner," Kyle says. "It's gonna be hot dogs and chips again, because that's pretty much all we got left."

"For somebody who plays a serial killer every night, you really are just the sweetest guy," I say. "I appreciate all your help. I know you were ready to get up outta here."

"Yeah, well, it's not like I have anything better to do," he says, smiling.

"I guess I don't get a compliment," Javier says.

I shrug. "I appreciate you too. Even if you get on my nerves."

He grins, and I suddenly remember what I saw on the monitor in the control center. "Hey, were you by any chance under the trapdoor in the boathouse a little while ago?"

Javier's brow furrows. "Today?" He shakes his head. "I've been asleep almost the whole time you were gone."

I turn to Kyle, and he shakes his head.

"I was cleaning out that nasty overflow fridge in the back," he says. "Why? What happened?"

"The camera that monitors the boathouse hatch kept going in and out," I say. "It came back on real quick, and I thought I saw something—someone—on the monitor."

"Ummmm," Kyle says nervously. "We were both in here the whole time you were gone. I swear."

"I believe you. I just—" I get up and walk around the breakfast bar, into the kitchen area, and kick aside the tattered rug that sits in front of the prep counter. The wooden floor slats run from left to right, and they're all a light oak color, but there is a square of flooring about three feet wide that's a shade darker than the rest. I crouch down and press the center board, and it flips up, revealing a small ring pull. Under the secret hatch is a tunnel that runs from the main lodge to the boathouse. We use it nightly to move Kyle from one place to another without the guests seeing him. It gives the illusion that he, much like the killers in *Friday the 13th* and *Halloween*, is always a step ahead and that he can appear and disappear at will. I reach down and grasp the pull.

"Wait, wait, wait," Bezi says, scrambling over and putting her hand on my shoulder. "What are you doing?"

"We should check and see if there's anything down there," I say.

"Hold up," Javier says. He goes to the closet and grabs a broom. He wields it like a sword, swinging it around in front of him. It makes a whooshing sound as he whips it through the air.

Kyle jumps back. "You wanna watch where you're swinging that thing? Damn." He edges around me and stands on the opposite side of the hatch. "What are you gonna do with that anyway?"

"Gotta be prepared," Javier says, without any hint that he's joking.

"To sweep the floor?" Bezi asks.

Javier spins the broom around in his hand, and Kyle ducks even though the broom isn't anywhere near him.

"Come on," I say. "I'll open the hatch on three."

Bezi grips my shoulder as Kyle balls his fists at his sides. Javier grips the broom so tight that his knuckles pale. I feel sorry for anything that might be down there, because we're either about to beat the shit out of an intruder or a defenseless raccoon.

I take a deep breath. "One . . . two . . . three!"

I yank up the hatch, and Javier brings the broom down on top of the open hatch like he's chopping wood. The handle flies so close to my face, I can feel the air brush my cheek. Kyle throws a wild haymaker and hits nothing but empty space. Bezi and I just stand there—absolutely nothing happens. There's nothing under the hatch.

"Good job, y'all," I say. "Thank you for protecting us from nothing."

Javier rolls his eyes. "A raccoon could have jumped out of there and attacked us."

"Doubtful," Bezi says.

"No," I say. "We had to fight a raccoon once." Me and Javier exchange knowing glances. "It's not a game. They're aggressive."

"Oh, okay," Bezi says, eyes wide. "Remind me to never come up here ever again."

I peer down into the opening in the floor. The tunnel is cut into the ground below and snakes off in the direction of the lake.

"Okay," I say. "Okay, let's go."

I grab the top rung of the rickety wooden ladder and lower myself down. It's a full twenty degrees colder down here, and a chill runs up my back. I strain in the inky dark to see the other end of the tunnel, but it's no use. I drag my hand along the wall until I find the little pull cord dangling near the hatch opening. I yank down on it, and three light bulbs flicker to life along the length of the ceiling. Even with the thready light from the bulbs, the other end is completely cloaked in darkness.

Bezi climbs down, followed by Javier, who's still clutching the broom handle. On the last rung, his foot slips and he stumbles, crashing to the ground at my feet. As he lands flat on his back, the air punches out of his lungs and he groans.

"Damn," I say, offering him my hand. "You okay?"

He scrambles to his feet and pretends to be fine.

"I'm good," he says through clenched teeth.

Kyle descends the ladder and has to stoop to keep from hitting his head. He looks Javier over, and the corners of his mouth lift. "What the hell, Javi?"

Javier is leaning on the broom, holding his breath like it hurts to breathe.

"Y'all come down here every night?" Bezi asks.

I grip her hand. "Kyle does. I come down here for maintenance checks, but that's usually in the mornings."

Kyle cups his hands around his mouth. "Hello?" he yells.

"Shhhhhut uuuppp!" Javier whisper-screams. "If there's somebody down here, you just announced our presence."

Kyle's face twists into an angry scowl. "I think hearing you fall through the hatch and the whole-ass conversation we just had already did that."

Javier huffs as I lead us down the cramped tunnel in the direction of the boathouse. It's damp and musty and the ceiling is too low. My heartbeat creeps up. I don't like the confined space. I have to keep telling myself that the walls are probably not closing in on me, but I don't know if I actually believe it. Everything suddenly feels too close, too dark.

It takes about ninety seconds to walk from one end of the tunnel to the other, and when we get to the hatch under the boathouse, we don't find some shadowy figure lurking in the dark or a raccoon. Just the hatch, and the slide bolt that keeps it locked, open.

"Didn't we lock this?" Kyle asks.

I nod. "Yeah. We always do. And look."

Scattered on the ground are little pieces of glass and black plastic. I take out my phone, turn on the flashlight, and sweep the column of light up to the security camera. The entire housing has been crushed, and what's left of it is hanging from its exposed wiring.

"Oh shit," Javier says. "It's broken."

It's not just broken. It's completely destroyed.

Bezi grips my arm. "I think we should get out of here."

A chill runs up my back, and it's not from the dank air sweeping through the underground tunnel. I grab Bezi's hand and go to push the hatch open when Javier yanks me back. Kyle puts his hand on my shoulder and presses his finger to his lips. His eyes are like empty sockets in the dark.

My heart thuds in my chest, but as I quiet myself, I hear a noise. The creak of a board just over my head.

Someone is standing directly on top of the hatch.

CHAPTER 10

I don't even breathe as the boards continue to creak. Bezi's fingertips dig into the skin on my forearm as a terrified grimace carves its way across her face. I press myself closer to her as we stare up through the boards. Dust from the floor above filters down.

Suddenly, Javier steps on the back of my heel as he shoves past me and takes off in the direction of the lodge. I grab Bezi by the hand and pull her along behind me as I race after him.

"Kyle!" I yell without looking back. "C'mon!"

I sprint down the tunnel, bumping my shoulder on the wall as I flail in the dark. I shove Bezi up the ladder and turn to see Kyle barreling toward me. I scramble up the ladder and Kyle follows. As soon as Kyle clears the hatch, I slam it closed. Kyle stumbles to his feet while Javier and Bezi drag a bunch of chairs and the coffee table over the top of the hatch to keep it shut. I quickly lock the front doors and pull the curtains closed.

"Who was that?" Javier asks as he struggles to catch his breath.

"Are we gonna talk about how you were gonna leave us to die?" Kyle says angrily. "I've never seen anybody run that fast."

"But did you die?" Javier asks.

"Everybody just calm down for a minute!" I say as I try to think straight. "Just wait. Okay. That security camera was smashed and somebody was definitely in the boathouse, right?"

Everyone nods in agreement.

"What is going on?" Bezi asks. "Do you think it was that lady—Ms. Keane?"

"Why would she come back?" I move to the window and peek through the curtains. "And if she's here, that means Porter, Tasha, and Paige won't find her at home. If she wasn't there, they should have come straight back." I have a clear view of the boathouse from the front window of the lodge.

Javier peers out the window beside me. "I don't see anybody."

I try to call Tasha, but I don't have a single bar's worth of reception. Shoving the phone back in my pocket, I look out the window again.

"Maybe it was a wild animal," Bezi offers.

Javier huffs. "Yeah, okay. A raccoon just happens to be standing on top of the hatch. What about the camera? A raccoon did that too?"

"I'm not saying it was a damn raccoon," Bezi says angrily. "I'm just saying. Who would do that? What for?"

A gust of wind blows through the pine trees, making their boughs rock and sway in the fading afternoon light. The front door of the boathouse bounces open as a blustery gale engulfs the structure. My heart pounds against my ribs so hard that it hurts, and my stomach sinks.

"You didn't lock it?" Javier asks.

I glance at him, then back to the boathouse. "I did."

With the door open, I can see that a decommissioned canoe has fallen out of its rack and is resting directly on top of the hatch.

Javier lets the air hiss out from between his teeth. "That explains that," Javier says. "We were running from a canoe. Nice."

"And the camera?" I ask. "And the lock on the boathouse? I know I locked it."

"You sure?" Kyle asks. "I forgot to lock the front gate. It's okay if it slipped your mind."

"No," I say adamantly. "I don't forget to do stuff like that."

Kyle's gaze traces down to the floor.

"Sorry," I say. "I'm not tryna make you feel bad. I'm just saying that I know I locked it."

Bezi tries to get Tasha on the phone, but she doesn't have a signal either.

"We gotta go to the office and use the landline," I say.

Javier's brows push up. "Who is 'we'? I'm not going anywhere."

"It's almost six," I say. "You're not worried about them?"

"Not really," says Javier. "They're probably on their way back right now."

Bezi crosses her arms over her chest. "I guess Tasha has a soft spot for insensitive jerks. Her last boyfriend was a lot like you. She dropped his sorry ass."

Javier shrugs. "Good thing I'm not her boyfriend, then, huh?"

Bezi and Javier look at each other like they want to fight.

"Stop," I say to both of them. "We're not going to argue. Not right now. I don't have a problem going to the office myself, but Tasha has a cell phone. Things might work on my end but they probably won't work on hers." There aren't any other choices, and as I weigh my options, I can see the light fading from the sky. "We gotta go get them."

"Again," Javier says. "Who is 'we'?"

I make sure my sneakers are knotted and I pull my hair up into a puff on top of my head. "Go. Or stay. I don't care what you do. I'm going to take a flashlight and go find them."

"I'm coming too," Bezi says.

Kyle sighs. "I guess I'm going too."

Javier glares at us. "You're just gonna leave me here? Alone?"

"Yeah," I say without hesitation.

He grumbles something I can't make out, then tilts his head and clenches his jaw. "Fine. We'll all go together."

Suddenly, my phone vibrates in my pocket, and I let out a little squeal as I scramble to pull it out. I breathe a sigh of relief as Tasha's name flashes across the screen.

I hit the green button and press the phone to my ear. "Tasha! Oh my god, where are you? I've been tryna call you, but the signal—"

Static garbles the line, and Tasha's voice breaks through in strangled yelps.

"Charity! . . . out there! I can't . . . please!"

Bezi grips my arm. "Where is she? What's happening?"

A fear unlike anything I've ever felt in my entire three years of working at Camp Mirror Lake, or my lifetime of horror-movie watching, grips my chest like a vise, squeezing it until I can barely breathe. I hold the phone away from my ear so that Bezi can hear what I'm hearing.

"Charity!" Tasha screams. ". . . gotta get away! . . . please . . ."

My breath hitches in my chest as I scream into the phone. "Tasha! Where are you? Tell me where you are!"

She's panting like she's running. Her ragged breaths tear through the line and embed themselves in my brain. "Help me!" she sobs. "Help . . . me . . ."

The line suddenly goes dead as the signal drops and a message flashes across the screen—"call failed." I stare at the phone in my hand like I'm not even holding it, like this isn't real.

"Oh my god," Bezi says in a whisper, her eyes brimming with tears. "She's out there."

"And something—something is happening." A knot claws its way up my throat. Her screams and sobs stick in my head. "We—we gotta go get her. Now."

I grab the extra flashlights we keep in the lodge closet and toss one to Javier, one to Kyle, one to Bezi. I turn mine on and off to make sure it works, then unlock the front door of the lodge. The early-evening sun slants through the trees, casting a hazy orange glow all around. The pine trees sway in the wind, and Mirror Lake watches silently.

"Do we even know where to go?" Javier asks.

"Porter said Ms. Keane's house was no more than two miles past mile marker sixty-eight," I say. "I know how to get out to that road, but I don't know if it's the same way Porter went. He knows the trail system better than me, but I think we should stick to the main road so we don't get lost."

"Should we drive?" Bezi asks. "We can take my car."

"We have to take the trail until we get to the main road," I say. "The car won't work back there."

Bezi takes a deep, wavering breath as she looks up at the sky. "We're going to be out there in the dark."

I grasp her hand. "Tasha is out there." I try to push away the sounds of her terrified screams and the thoughts of what might have caused her to sound that way. "We stay together. We move fast. No side trips. We go to the last place we know Tasha was headed; then we regroup and decide what to do from there. Agreed?"

Bezi, Kyle, and even Javier nod.

• • •

The path that twists around behind the supply shed isn't maintained as well as the other paths that snake through Camp

Mirror Lake. It's overgrown with spider grass, and the gravel is heaped in uneven treads. Mr. Lamont mentioned that it used to extend all the way to Route 710 but that access was abandoned for the main entrance years ago.

The trees press in on us from either side of the trail, and the darkness descends like a shade being drawn across the sky. Kyle clicks on his flashlight. I save the battery on mine, figuring we'll need it for the walk back. The trail continues through the trees, and while a tall gate bars our path, I can see that it continues into a thickly wooded area. A rusted chain is looped through the gate, and it's secured with a large, equally rusted padlock. I yank on it, and bits of orange metal flake off on my palm.

"Great," Javier says. "A little tetanus on the way to meet a shotgun-wielding recluse. This was such a good idea, Charity."

I ignore Javier and push on the gate. The chain is only loosely securing the entrance, and by pushing hard, a gap opens, and we slip through.

"Come on," I say, gesturing for Bezi to go through.

She squeezes in and pops out the other side, then holds the gate open so I can slip through after her. We pry the gate apart for Javier and for Kyle, and when we're all through, I survey the path ahead. The dark is almost complete now, and long shadows lean across the uneven pathway. Snaps and clicks sound from the surrounding forest. The feeling of being watched from the deepening shadows stokes a sense of panic in me. I feel like I can't quite catch my breath or make my heart slow down. I have to beat back the fear over and over again as we push forward.

"This was such a bad idea," Javier whines as he steps on the back of my heel.

I round on him. "I know we said we were gonna stick together, but damn. Can you watch my foot?"

"I'm scared," he says, his voice cracking. "There are bears and shit out here, Charity. You think that's what Tasha was talking about?"

I don't answer him. All I want to do is find Tasha, and if I think too long about what was making her sound that way on the phone, I might lose my nerve. I turn back around and, keeping a firm grip on Bezi's hand, lead us to the end of the path that intersects Route 710 in what I guess is about the length of a couple of city blocks. The paved road is crumbling, and vining foliage runs along the cracks. It doesn't look like it's being maintained at all.

"This way leads to the next mile marker," I say, gesturing to the right.

"Two miles in the dark?" Javier asks. "No streetlights. Nothing. Just us and these weak-ass flashlights?"

"Maybe we'll run into Tasha or the others on the way there," Kyle offers.

I hope so. The less time we have to spend out here the better.

"We should go back," Javier says. "They never should've come out here in the first place."

All the frustration and fear that has been building in me spills out. "Stay or go! I don't care! Maybe you don't care about anybody but yourself, but my friends are out there, so get your shit together or get out of my face."

Javier shrinks away from me. "Damn," he says. "Sorry."

Kyle shines his light down the road. The dark swallows the cone of pale yellow light like a giant, gaping mouth. I still myself, willing my heart to find a pace that doesn't feel like I've had ten energy drinks. Outside the perimeter of the camp, without the comforts of my cabin or the routine of the nightly game, I feel painfully exposed. Tasha's frantic, broken words stick in my head. I push on with Bezi at my heel and Kyle and Javier trailing behind. I have to find my friends.

Thirty-five minutes later, the light from Kyle's flashlight illuminates mile marker seventy.

"Look for a driveway or something," I say, switching on my flashlight. The beam barely puts a dent in the darkness surrounding us, but I sweep it along the side of the main road, looking for any indication that Ms. Keane's residence is somewhere nearby.

"Over here," Javier says after a few minutes.

He's got his light on and pointed at a splintered wooden post with the numbers 5980 scrawled on the side in reflective white paint. It looks like a mailbox was affixed to the top at some point, but it's nowhere to be seen. Beyond it are two tracks that look like they'd line up with car tires, but to call it a driveway would be a stretch. It's just the remnant of an unpaved road snaking into the forest. Stuck in the ground is a makeshift wooden sign with the words NO TRESPASSING drawn on in red spray paint.

"You gotta be kidding me," Bezi says. "This is it? I don't even see a house."

"It's probably way back in the trees," I say as I try to peer through the tree cover.

Kyle points his light in the direction of the tracks, and still I see nothing. I grip my own flashlight and walk onto the road. Bezi lays her hand against my back as she follows me up the drive. Kyle and Javier stay close behind.

NO TRESPASSING signs line the drive on both sides, a repeated warning that begs me not to ignore it. After several minutes of trudging up the narrow drive, we see a muted light coming from a window on the upper floor of a house situated in a thick grove of towering pines. Javier stops dead in his tracks, his flashlight pointed at the ground.

"Oh my god, come on!" I say angrily. "You are not gonna—"

"Look," Javier whispers.

The beam from his flashlight is hovering over something on the ground. I crouch down and poke at it. It's caked in mud, but the bubble-gum-pink fabric underneath is unmistakable— it's Tasha's hair tie.

I snatch it up. "She was here," I say. "Good. That means this lady—Ms. Keane—probably saw her and can tell us how long ago she left."

"She probably got turned around in the dark," Kyle says.

"But she's with Porter," Javier says. "He doesn't really get turned around out here."

I move toward the house, and Kyle steps into my path.

I gaze up at him. "What is it?"

"I just— Something isn't right. I don't like this." Fear is plastered across his face like a mask.

I gently touch his arm. "We gotta find them. As soon as we talk to this lady, we can go."

He sighs, gives me a quick nod, and we continue on to the house.

. . .

The front yard is littered with trash, plastic pink flamingos stuck in the ground. Some of their legs and beaks are missing. Several burned-out vehicles are scattered across the front of the property. Even in the dark, I can see the splintering wood and curling paint on the main house. There are gaps in the siding and the roof is partially covered with a big blue tarp held in place by bungee cords and broken cinder blocks. The screens are caked with dirt, and from the sound of it, there is a colony of cats living under the dilapidated front porch.

"You seen *Texas Chainsaw Massacre?*" Javier whispers.

"This is not the time," Bezi says through clenched teeth. "Shut up."

I can't see Javier's face in the dark, but I can almost feel him roll his eyes.

I climb the front steps, praying that they won't collapse

under me, and ring the bell. After a few moments and no answer, I knock. From inside, there's a muffled shuffle.

Footsteps.

I hold my breath and try to rehearse what I'm going to say.

"Remember me? You threatened me with a shotgun, but it's fine. I'm looking for my friends."

The door creaks open just enough for someone on the other side to peer out at me.

"Who's there?" she asks.

There's no mistaking the voice. It's the same one that was yelling at me the previous morning.

"Ms. Keane," I say in my most polite, sickly-sweet voice. "Ms. Keane, my name is Charity. I'm so sorry to bother you, but—"

"Didn't you see the signs?" she asks, pulling the door open a little more. Her tone mirrors my own—very sweet and very fake. It immediately sets something off in my gut. It's almost like she's mocking me.

"The trespassing signs?" I ask. "I'm sorry. I saw them, but I'm looking for my friends, and I know they came this way."

"Do you now?" She pulls the door all the way open but keeps her right hand behind the door itself. "And how do you know that? I haven't seen anybody."

"You didn't see anyone?" I ask. Tasha's hair tie is in my pocket. She was here. "You're sure? Please, Ms. Keane. I know what happened with you at the camp was probably just a misunderstanding." I hate placating her this way, but it feels like it's my only hope of getting any information out of her. "Please. We could really use your help."

There's a soft click, and before I can move away from the door, Ms. Keane levels her shotgun at my head. I stare down the barrel, and there's a noise from over my shoulder, a gasp as Bezi and the others register what I'm seeing.

"Get in here," Ms. Keane says.

My body begins to tremble so violently, I have to grab hold of the doorframe to keep myself from collapsing. The rush of blood in my ears blurs the noises around me.

"Now," she says. She glances past me. "You too. Get in here."

I walk on unsteady legs into the living room of Ms. Keane's house. It smells like dust and cat urine. Every square inch of the place is covered in trash. Framed pictures of Jesus hang crooked on the walls, and dozens of cats prance around like they own the place. Bezi and Javier follow me inside. I wait for Kyle to follow, but as I glance back, I realize he's not there. Ms. Keane slams the door shut and waves the shotgun around in front of me. I wince every time the barrel whizzes past my face.

"Can't leave well enough alone," Ms. Keane mumbles. "Sit down."

No one moves.

She pumps the shotgun once and levels it at me again. We all sit on a musty cat-hair-covered couch as she paces in front of us.

"Lemonade?" she asks.

"Wha—what?" Javier stammers.

"Lem-on-ade," she repeats, emphasizing every syllable. "Thirsty?"

"I— No," I say.

I don't think even the threat of catching a bullet could get me to drink or eat anything from inside this house. Ms. Keane turns her back to us and lets the gun rest on her hip but keeps her finger close to the trigger.

"Is she seriously offering us drinks?" Bezi whispers against my ear.

Ms. Keane spins around, and I wince as she points the firearm at us again. "It's the polite thing to do when you have guests, you know. Offer food, drinks. I'm a little rusty. Don't have many visitors but I have some lemonade."

Javier stifles a gag. "I think we're good."

"Ah well." Ms. Keane sighs as she sits down in a rocking chair directly across from us. She rests the butt of the gun on the floor. "You're the kids from the camp." She sucks her teeth. Her ragged salt-and-pepper hair is hanging around her face like a shroud, but her eyes, black as coal, stand out. "I don't like it. Not one little bit. It's not the way things should be."

"I don't know what you mean, but I want to," I say. I try sucking up to her again. "I'm looking for my friends. They came out here to talk to you about the camp, about its history. We really want to understand, and they figured you'd be the best person to ask."

Her beady eyes narrow and her mouth turns down. "Its history?" Her unkempt brows push up. "What do you know about it? Can't be too much or you wouldn't be here."

I try to judge how quickly I can get to the door, but Ms. Keane is positioned almost directly between it and us.

"Well, that's what my friends came here to find out," I say as I fight to keep my voice steady. "I heard what you said, Ms. Keane. You said we should be ashamed of ourselves, that if we knew what you know, it might mean something. What did you mean by that?"

Ms. Keane rocks back and looks up at the ceiling but keeps her fingers curled around the barrel of the shotgun. "That camp is an abomination. Distasteful if you ask me." She raises her face to the ceiling again.

"How?" I ask. "We don't know what you mean." I glance at Javier, who looks down into his lap.

Bezi slides her hand onto my leg and squeezes it. Hard. Her eyes are wide, and I realize she's trying to get me to look at something in her line of sight. I follow her gaze to a window at the front of the house. Kyle's shadowy silhouette is hovering behind the glass. He's wildly gesturing to the side of the house, but I can't make out what he's trying to tell me. Ms. Keane raises her head and I immediately lower my gaze to the floor.

"Did you know that this place is special?" she asks. Her voice has a hollow, faraway tone, like she's completely disconnected from the fact that she's holding us hostage. "It's old. Used to be a glacier lying over the whole place. That's why you have all these lakes. After the ice melted, the ground opened up like a bunch of starving mouths." She pauses for a moment before continuing. "Don't think *they* were out here when the land was all ice and snow, but the land was here. Sleeping under the ice."

I glance at Bezi, who has a look of utter confusion plastered across her face.

"Who is 'they'?" I ask.

Ms. Keane stares at me for a moment without speaking. I feel my stomach drop. I wonder if I've made a mistake by asking questions, but she slips back into her rambling.

"They didn't used to have a name at all, I don't think." She pushes a loose strand of her greasy hair behind her ear. "Now they're owls."

Javier makes a small grunt, and Ms. Keane shifts the gun from one hand to the other and back again.

"Ever wonder how people come to power?" she asks in a way that tells me she doesn't expect me to answer. "Seems so random sometimes, doesn't it? How does a man like that become president? How does a person like that accumulate so much wealth? How does it all just seem to fall in place for some folks? Especially the ones who don't deserve it." She barks out a sickly sounding laugh, the phlegm snapping in the back of her throat like a firecracker. "No coincidences there, honey. Just knowledge of things regular everyday folk don't have."

"What's that mean?" Bezi asks. "What kind of knowledge?"

Ms. Keane coughs into her curled fist and wipes whatever came out across the front of her dress. "There are things in this world that aren't meant for everybody. These people, they knew that. Knew they couldn't just have their secrets blowing in the wind." She sighs but keeps her finger on the trigger of the shotgun. "The words, the things they do, let them be and do whatever they want. Politicians, movie stars, richest people in the world—they all get what they want because they're willing to do whatever it takes. Even if that means spilling a little blood."

My heart nearly stops. Bezi's leg trembles against mine, and I put my hand on her knee.

"An owl as big as a man roams these woods," Ms. Keane says. "Feathers white as a fresh snow, eyes like black glass." She laughs. "Those people out there, they know about it. They named their whole order after it. Ran all their business out of that big lodge out past the grove. They know about this place, this land, the things it can give you if you're willing to feed it. Nobody would ever believe it." She looks me dead in the face. "But they should."

"Does that have something to do with the campers who died out here back in the seventies?" I ask, trying to keep her talking. "We thought maybe you knew something about that summer camp that used to be out here." Keep her talking. Keep her attention on something other than shooting us.

Ms. Keane smiles. "What happened to them was a misstep. But the others . . . well, the owl got them."

"Others," Bezi whispers.

Ms. Keane smiles, but there is nothing but malice behind her eyes.

"The owl," I say. "What's that?"

Ms. Keane leans forward in her chair. She grins, and her mouth is like a void as the thin lips pull back over her teeth. "Oh, honey. You're going to die out here, and there's not a damn thing you can do about it."

I clench my jaw and grip Bezi's knee. I think if I rush Ms. Keane, she'll shoot me, but maybe it'll give Bezi and Javier a chance to get away.

Ms. Keane readjusts the gun on her lap, and I steal a quick glance at the window. Kyle isn't there anymore. My heart ticks up as Ms. Keane runs her withered finger over the barrel of the gun.

"Please," I say as panic grips me. "We just want to find our friends. If you say you haven't seen them, we believe you."

Javier nods enthusiastically.

"And we can just leave you alone," Bezi says. "We never meant to bother you."

"Well, you did," Ms. Keane says. "And I'm sorry, honey, but I can't let that go unpunished."

I try to slow my breathing. I'm going to grab the lamp that's perched on the table next to me. The shade is dusty and the bulb flickers on and off, but the base looks solid, like it's made of brass or something. If I can get close enough to Ms. Keane, I might be able to knock her out or at least incapacitate her with it.

"If only they had been more open," Ms. Keane says. "They could have shared what they knew and then maybe things wouldn't have gone so terribly wrong." She huffs. "But now you're here. So what am I supposed to do?"

Every muscle in my body tenses as she rambles. I move my elbow to the armrest, trying to shorten the distance between my hand and the lamp. Ms. Keane becomes more and more agitated as the seconds tick by. She pulls at her dress with one hand while gripping the gun with the other.

"Nobody listens!" she snaps. "They all want power, but they don't know what to do with it. They think they're better than us. Please."

From the rear of the house, there's a calamitous crash. I jump up, and Ms. Keane turns to look into the kitchen. I grab the lamp, feel its weight in my hand. Half the room is swallowed by the dark as I yank the cord from the wall. I take two steps forward, raise the lamp, and bring it down on top of Ms. Keane's head, where it lands with a sickening crack.

The shade pops off the lamp and skids across the floor as Ms. Keane lets out a pained gasp and staggers forward. I raise the lamp again and bring it down, but she turns her body so that I only manage to catch her shoulder. She drops her gun and howls in pain. I throw the lamp at her as hard as I can and turn just in time to see Javier sprinting out the front door. I grab Bezi and pull her toward the door just as Ms. Keane finds her shotgun on the floor. She swings it up, cursing and sputtering, a line of blood-tinged spittle hanging from her bottom lip. Her shoulder is sloped in a way that tells me it's either broken or dislocated. She struggles to get the gun under her control.

We're out the front door and sprinting down the drive in a blink. Javier stumbles but doesn't let himself fall as he runs ahead of us. We're halfway down the drive when a gunshot splits the air like a bolt of lightning. I throw myself face-first into the dirt, and Bezi falls beside me. A sharp pain rockets through my knee as it strikes the ground. Another shot rings out and splinters a tree just off the driveway to our right.

"She's shooting at us!" Javier screams. "Get up! Go!"

We scramble to our feet and keep running. I ignore the pain in my knee. I keep moving even though it feels like I'm trudging through quicksand. As we get to the crest in the driveway, I slide to a grinding halt.

A tall figure stands at the bottom of the drive near the road.

Another gunshot ricochets through the trees.

The figure stalks toward us, and I panic. We can't go back. We can't go forward. I step toward the trees as Javier lights the figure up with his flashlight and, in a rush of relief, I realize it's Kyle.

"Come on!" he yells. "We gotta get out of here!"

I've never been much of an athlete. I passed gym with a C-plus, but I run the entire two miles back to the rear entrance of the camp without stopping. I ignore the ache in my calves and the burning in my lungs. Each time Bezi tries to stop to catch her breath, I pull her forward. We don't have time to be winded or tired.

At the rear gate, we squeeze through the opening as quickly as we can. As soon as we're safely inside the fence, I race toward the office. I want to call the sheriff, but a part of me feels like he won't even care. Still, I have to get ahold of somebody. Anybody. We need help.

"The office!" I say, gasping. "We gotta call—"

I'm moving past the Western Lodge when something catches my eye. Some subtle movement I realize is coming from inside the lodge itself. I come to a full stop for the first time since we left Ms. Keane's property. The lodge doors are sitting wide open. The fluorescent lights in the kitchen are on, and they're casting a cold glow throughout the main hall. Standing in front of the unlit fireplace is a person.

Bezi is panting beside me when Kyle and Javier notice the figure too. I nearly stop breathing as a sudden chill runs up my back and settles in the nape of my neck. I take a step toward the open doors, blinking, unable to fully comprehend what I'm seeing.

The stooped figure is standing with their back to me. They are barefoot, shirtless, and they have their arms wrapped around their own waist as if they're trying to hold themselves together. Their skin is caked with mud and something else— something dark smeared across their arms and the naked skin of their back.

I take the steps slowly, one at a time, listening to the figure as ragged breaths tear out of them. From the porch, I peer in at the person.

"H-hello?" I call out. I immediately kick myself. Paige would tell me that my Black ass has no business calling out in the dark to a stranger. I'm sure that's against the rules.

They turn to face me and I let out a strangled yelp as I realize this is no stranger. I know this person.

CHAPTER 11

Tasha.

She tilts her head, and her gaze flits to me and then to the others. She turns her attention back to the fireplace without uttering a single word. I rush forward, my arms outstretched. But she doesn't reach for me. As soon as I touch her, a long, agonized cry escapes her throat, and then a terrible silence engulfs us.

Bezi rushes up, but I wave her away and slowly put my hands up in front of me. I take one step forward.

"Tasha. It's okay. It's me. It's Charity."

She steps back, and her bare feet against the wooden floor make a wet sound. That dark substance smeared across her body is blood, and her bare feet are trailing it across the floor. She holds her stomach with her bloodied hands.

I approach her slowly, speaking softly. "Tasha?" I whisper. I try to keep my voice calm, but I'm failing. "Tasha. I'm here. You're safe now. What—what happened to you?"

"Char—Charity?" she asks like she's unsure she recognizes me—one of her oldest friends. Her voice is hoarse, like she's been crying or screaming for hours.

She angles herself toward me. The light from the kitchen illuminates the part of her body that had been in shadow, and I'm so utterly horrified by her horrendous injuries that I have to stifle the urge to vomit. Her right eye is swollen shut, the lid purple and bulging like the orb is trying to escape its socket. Blood and dirt are smeared across her entire face. Her bottom lip is split clean open, the pulpy pink insides pushing out. Her hair is caked with mud, and it's hard to tell, but I think she's missing some teeth.

I slowly put my hands on her bare arms as she holds them close to her body. She tenses at first, then relaxes just enough for me to see a long horizontal gash to her belly, and even though it's caked with mud and bits of leaves and dead grass, I see something fleshy and pink and wet beneath. My heart sinks. Her insides are showing through the injury, and I'm having trouble understanding how she's alive, much less on her feet.

Bezi clamps her hand over her mouth, stifling a sob. Kyle grabs a blanket from the couch and slips it around Tasha's bare shoulders. She doesn't flinch away or cry out, just tilts her head back and looks up at the ceiling. I grab the edges of the blanket and pull it closed in front of her, covering her horrible injury as if that will make it go away.

"What happened to you?" I ask again.

Tasha wobbles and as her legs buckle, Javier swoops in and catches her before she hits the floor. I grab her legs and help him lower her onto the couch. Her chest rises and falls in an erratic pattern, and a halting rasp gurgles from her throat.

"What the hell happened to her?" Javier asks as he kneels at her side, his hands trembling as he props a pillow under Tasha's head.

Kyle rushes to the lodge doors and locks them. I eye the pile of chairs over the secret hatch in the kitchen.

"They're right where we left them," Kyle says, following my gaze.

"We gotta call the police," Bezi says as she dabs at Tasha's face with the sleeve of her sweatshirt.

"I—I think she's in shock or something," I say.

"No shit!" Javier says. "You see her stomach?"

"Shut up!" Bezi says through broken sobs. "Don't talk about it." She puts her hand on Tasha's forehead. "Tasha, babes, you're gonna be fine. I promise. Just hold on. We're gonna get you some help."

I take out my phone, but I already know what I'm going to see. "I don't have a signal." Tasha's blood sticks under my nails, and my hands are shaking so bad, I can barely keep hold of my phone. "We have to go to the office to make the call from the landline."

"No," Tasha whispers.

I lean over her and gently take her face in my hands. "What? Tasha, what happened? We gotta get you some help."

"No," she says without looking at me. "Don't . . . go. It's— it's out there."

"What?" I lean in and put my ear close to her mouth to try and catch every word. The smell of blood and dirt wafts off her and turns my stomach over. "What's out there?"

"The . . . the . . . the owl." Tasha's one visible eye rolls back until only the white part is showing. Her breathing becomes shallow.

"The owl," I repeat.

"Ms. Keane was talking about an owl," Javier says.

Bezi nods. "What are we going to do?"

"We can drive out now, right?" Javier asks.

Bezi perks up. "Get my keys out of my bag. We'll take my car."

Javier rushes to Bezi's bag and dumps it on the floor. Kyle joins him and helps paw through the stuff.

"Where are they?" Kyle asks frantically. "Bezi, the keys. I can't find them."

Bezi leaves Tasha's side and searches around in her bag, turning it inside out.

"I—I must have left them in the cabin?" she stammers in a haze of confusion.

"We cleared the cabins," I say. The hair on the back of my neck stands on end. "Check your pockets," I say as panic grips me. "Check the bag again!"

Unconscious, Tasha whimpers. I squeeze her hand. Something isn't right, but we don't have time to figure it out. *Tasha* doesn't have time.

"Tasha?" I say gently. But it's no use. She's completely out of it. "We have to call an ambulance. Everybody, check your phones. Anybody have a signal?"

We all check our phones.

"I got one bar!" Bezi squeals. She immediately dials 911.

I hold my breath, praying that the call will connect.

"Hello?" Bezi says frantically as she practically jumps up and down in relief. "Hello? We need help! We're at Camp Mirror Lake. Please!" She pauses and her brows push together. "What? Hello? No. Mirror Lake. The camp! Please!" She holds the phone away from her face, and tears fill her eyes. "The call dropped."

"Do you think they heard anything you said?" Kyle asks. "Will they send somebody?"

"I—I don't know," Bezi says.

Kyle slumps onto the recliner with his head in his hands. "This cannot be happening."

Javier moves toward the door, slipping on his coat. "I'm going to the office to call an ambulance from the landline."

Kyle looks up. "Whoever did that to her is still out there, and you're just gonna go for a fuckin' stroll?"

"What else are we supposed to do?" Javier asks angrily. "Just let her die?"

Kyle shakes his head. "No. But—"

"But nothing," Javier says. "I'd go look for Bezi's keys, but I feel like I'd be wasting time. I'm going to the office. You all keep looking. I'll be right back."

For the first time in the last few days, it seems like he's genuinely concerned about somebody other than himself.

"I'll go with you," Bezi says.

I start to protest, but Javier beats me to it.

"Nah," he says. "I'll be okay. Stay with her." He moves to the front window and peers out into the dark. "I'll take a flashlight. Once I'm inside with the door locked, I'll flash the light on and off three times; that way you know I'm safe. I'll call an ambulance and the police; then we'll all get outta here and never come back. Sound like a plan?"

I nod as Javier slips a flashlight in his pocket and tenses his entire body like he's getting ready to run a race. Kyle gets up and opens the door for him, and Javier bolts down the steps, disappearing into the dark. Kyle slams the door shut, locking it, and I crane my neck at the window to try and track Javier. I see the reflective yellow stripe on the back of his coat as he books it to the front office. A few moments later, three flashes come from the window and I exhale a sigh of relief.

"He's in," I say. "He's safe."

Tasha stirs, and I rush to her side as Bezi takes hold of her hand. Tasha groans, and her hands open and close into fists.

"I know it hurts," Bezi says. "Try not to move too much."

I grab a stack of hand towels from the kitchen and bring them back to the couch. I gently lift the blanket covering Tasha's belly. A terrible sinking feeling settles over me as I get a good look at the wound. I make my face a mask, but inside I want to scream. I press the towels against the wound, and Tasha groans.

Tasha is dying.

If we don't get her some help soon, she is not going to make it.

"Por—Porter and Paige," Tasha whispers through her swollen and bloodied lips. Her eye flutters open, and she tries to turn over, but the pain steals her breath, and she rests her head back against the couch cushion.

"Where are they?" I ask gently. "Tasha, please. What happened to them?"

"They—they're out. They're still out there."

"Where?" I ask. "Where are they, Tasha? You went to Ms. Keane's house, right?"

She nods, then winces. "Somebody was watching. We ran . . . the other way. The trees . . . were . . . black. Little owls . . . on the trunk." She takes a deep, wavering breath. "Then there was—this place. In the trees." She grips my arm. "The owl. It's killing us."

She lapses into unconsciousness and I sit back, my throat tight, my mind racing.

"Paige and Porter are out there," Bezi says. "If the same thing that happened to Tasha is happening to them, Charity . . ." She covers her mouth with trembling fingers.

She doesn't have to say anything else. I'm sure I'm thinking the same thing she is. Paige is our friend and so is Porter. They are in trouble, and whatever happened to Tasha wasn't an accident. Somebody did that to her, and our friends are still out there.

I go back to the window and look toward the office. I can see the glow from Javier's flashlight bouncing around inside, but I can't see him. He's had plenty of time to make the call.

"Help is on the way," I say. "But I don't think I can wait. Paige and Porter are out there right now."

"What are you saying?" Kyle asks. "You want to go back out there?"

Bezi looks at me quizzically. "Charity, I know you wanna help, but maybe we should wait for the police."

"Paige and Porter can't wait," I say, feeling like I don't have any good options left. "It's gonna take forty minutes for the police to get up here and then who knows how long to organize a search. We don't have that kind of time."

Bezi shakes her head. "We don't even know who or what is out there. Why does Tasha keep talking about an owl? And Ms. Keane said the same thing. What does that even mean?"

I slip a flashlight into my pocket and pull on a cardigan. "I don't know. But I'm going."

Bezi jumps up. "You can't go alone."

I turn to Kyle, who looks like he's about to be sick.

"You stay here with Tasha until Javier comes back and the ambulance shows up, okay?" I say to Kyle. "Keep the doors locked and stay away from the windows."

"This is a bad idea," he says.

"I know," I say. "But I don't have any better choices."

"Just stay here till Javier gets back," Kyle says. He's on the verge of tears. "Please just stay."

I squeeze his arm. "We'll be okay. We're gonna retrace Tasha's steps, but we're not going anywhere near Ms. Keane's property. Tasha said they went the other way, so I'm thinking they continued on toward the next mile marker. We'll go see what we can find and get back here as soon as we can. When the ambulance shows up, just go with Tasha and Javier to the hospital, okay?"

He shakes his head and stands up. "No. I want to stay and make sure you come back."

"No," I say firmly. "Get Tasha out of here. Don't wait for us. Just tell the police where we went and send them after us. Hopefully we'll run into them on the way back."

Kyle leans down and gives me a hug, and I can feel his heart pounding out of his chest. I move toward the door, and as Kyle unlocks it, I glance back at Tasha.

"I got her," Kyle says. "Please. Be careful."

Bezi and I go out onto the front steps. I glance toward the office, and Javier's light is gone from the window.

"Let's go," I say to Bezi. "I want to find them and get back."

We sprint to the path behind the supply shed, squeeze through the gate, and make our way down Route 710.

• • •

As we approach mile marker seventy, we turn off our flashlights and move in absolute silence as Ms. Keane's partially obscured driveway comes into view. My heart rattles around in my chest as a thin film of sweat blankets my brow. We've been alternating between running and walking, trying to get to wherever it is we're going as fast as possible. As we approach Ms. Keane's drive, I struggle to keep my breaths quiet.

Bezi grabs hold of my jacket as we stay close to the tree line on the opposite side of the road. When we clear the immediate area, we switch on our flashlights and continue on.

I've never been so far down Route 710. In my mind, I expect that it will continue for miles and miles into the vast wilderness beyond Camp Mirror Lake, but as we pass mile marker seventy-one, the paved road comes to an abrupt end. The broken concrete crumbles away and transitions into a flat stretch of dirt road littered with fallen trees and overgrown underbrush.

"You think they would have gone that way?" I ask, shining my light into the trees. I squat down and try to catch my breath. "What do we do? They could have kept going, right? They're on foot, so maybe they went that way? A car couldn't make it but on foot . . . maybe."

I turn to Bezi, who's pointing her light into the trees just to the right of the main road.

"Bezi?" I ask.

She's got her light trained on a single tree. It's an oak, but its trunk is so black that it looks like a void in the already darkened forest. There is something carved into the base of the tree. I swing my light to the same spot and see a pair of carved eyes staring back at me.

"What is that?" Bezi asks.

I move closer to examine the carving and find that the blackened bark of the tree isn't natural. Some kind of pigment coats the trunk from the root to about twelve feet off the ground. I run my hand over the bark.

"I think it's paint," I say.

Near the base, the pale inner flesh of the tree is exposed where a small owl is carved. Its features are worn but it's clearly an owl—the oversize eyes, hint of a beak, wings tucked close to its sides.

Something stirs in the deepest part of my memory—that place where only images exist and not in a way that makes any real sense. In my mind's eye, I see the painted face of an owl. It's in a sketchbook done in pencil. There's someone there and then—nothing.

"You okay?" Bezi asks.

I shake my head, and the images dissolve like smoke in the open air.

"I think I've seen this before."

Bezi's brows push up. "What? Where?"

"I don't know. I can't remember."

Bezi and I stand in silence for a moment before I decide it doesn't matter.

Bezi crouches down and runs her fingers over the carving. "What do you think it means?"

"No clue," I say. I sweep the light around, and it falls on a path about the width of a sidewalk that leads directly into the woods behind the tree with the owl carving.

"Where do you think that goes?" Bezi asks.

"I don't know, but if Tasha and the others got turned around out here, maybe she followed the path? She mentioned the owls. This has to be the way she went."

Bezi shrugs. "I don't want *us* to get lost. You might be the final girl, but that's not really making me feel better right now."

I grasp her hand. "If you wanna go back, I understand."

Bezi shakes her head. "I'm not leaving you. Me and you till the end of the world, right?"

I kiss her gently on the cheek, taking just the smallest pause to feel the tenderness of this moment. I have a terrible feeling about what lies ahead, but Bezi and I are in this together, to whatever end.

We keep our fingers laced together as we step onto the path. The forest is a black void on either side of the trail. The noises echoing out are familiar—the beating of bird wings, the scurrying of tiny feet through the underbrush. But every few yards, there is a break deep in the woods where the light from my flashlight cannot reach. I tell myself it's a deer, a fox, something that belongs here and not the images my mind has conjured of some unnaturally large birdlike creature. Bezi is squeezing my hand so hard that my bones ache, but I don't say anything. The pain keeps me alert, reminds me that I'm out here with one thing to do—find Porter and Paige.

We trudge down the trail for thirty minutes before coming to another oak tree whose trunk has been painted black, a small owl carved at the base. Another trail extends beyond it, snaking off into the blackness.

"Somebody put these carvings here," Bezi whispers. "Why?"

"I think they're like the mile markers on the road," I say as we push on down the new stretch of pathway. "Like guideposts or something."

"Leading where?" Bezi asks.

I shrug. "I don't know, but Tasha was out here, running from something, and she was terrified. She was injured so bad. *Something* happened. I just—" I suddenly feel like I can see a little farther into the trees. I can see a little more of the night sky overhead. "The trees are thinning."

Ahead, there's a flickering orange light. I gently squeeze Bezi's arm and quietly lead her off the path into the cover of the trees. I click off my flashlight and press my finger to my lips in a plea for silence. Bezi covers her mouth with her hands and crouches down as I switch off her flashlight for her. Just ahead, there is a clearing and what looks like some kind of wooden platform illuminated by a large torch.

"Somebody is out here," I whisper against Bezi's ear.

Keeping close to the ground, I inch forward, crawling on my stomach across the dirt and dead leaves. After a few minutes, I have a clear view of the opening among the trees. It's a large open airspace. A wooden platform in the shape of a crescent stands beneath a massive oak tree. It reminds me of an outdoor amphitheater. Opposite the stagelike platform are three tiers of wooden risers—seating for at least a hundred people.

I press myself flat against the ground as Bezi crawls up beside me.

"What is this place?" I ask.

Bezi shrugs and sinks lower in the brush. We watch in complete silence for several long minutes. There is no movement, no sound, and after a while, I slowly stand up.

"What are you doing?" Bezi whisper-yells. "Get down!"

I'm only thinking about how much time we've already wasted by hiding in the bushes. Porter and Paige can't wait around for us to work up the courage to find them.

"Come on."

The flashlight stays off as I lead Bezi out of the brush and into the open space ahead. The path leads us right into it. The blazing torch casts a hazy orange glow all around. I scan the area again, listening. There's no one here, but somebody had to have been, and recently. The torch snaps and crackles as the fire consumes the end of it.

"Charity," Bezi says, her voice nothing more than a whisper. "We shouldn't be here. This is all wrong."

I climb onto the crescent-shaped platform and walk from one side to the other. The trunk of the giant oak that stands directly behind it is carved—a pattern of overlapping triangular eaves. The torchlight illuminates only the very bottom part of the tree, so I switch on my flashlight and swing the light up where a pair of shining black eyes stares back at me. I stumble back and Bezi gasps. The tree trunk has been carved into the likeness of a giant owl. It looms over us. Set in its eye sockets are polished black stones, and the firelight reflected in them gives them a lifelike appearance. Part of me wonders if it's alive, if this is the figure Ms. Keane spoke of. I picture it opening its pointed beak, grasping me in its taloned claws.

A shudder runs through my body, and as I step back to take in the entirety of the massive carving, my foot nearly slips out from under me. I steady myself and point my flashlight at the wooden planks beneath my sneakers.

"It's wet," I say. "This whole area right here." I crouch down and touch the damp planks, a watery substance coating my fingers, and as I examine it in the light, I'm almost 100 percent sure it's blood that somebody has tried to clean up by flooding the area with water.

"Look," Bezi says. She's got her light pointed at another path that snakes off the opposite side of the outdoor amphitheater.

I wipe my hands on my jeans and march toward the path with Bezi at my heel. This pathway is paved and much narrower than the others. The trees and shrubbery that run alongside it are neatly trimmed.

Ahead, a large structure unfolds out of the darkness. Bezi and I find ourselves in the shadow of a massive lodge.

Three stories high, it looks similar to the Western Lodge but is triple the size, and its entrance is flanked by two massive carved owls. The upper windows are dark and some are boarded up. A tangle of twisted thorny vines snakes its way up the facade of the building. The path leading to the front steps is smooth and even. Lying directly in the center of it is a shoe.

I rush forward and snatch it up. It's covered in mud and the laces are undone, but I recognize it as soon as I wipe it off with the hem of my shirt. It's a red sneaker with a yellow swoosh on the side.

"Porter."

I take a step toward the building, but Bezi grabs my arm and pulls me back.

"We cannot go in there," she says.

"Why not?"

Bezi shakes her head. "Think about what happened to Tasha. Maybe the person who did that to her is in there. What do you think they'll do to us? Nah. We gotta get out of here and get some help."

"We don't have time to go back. We're here right now." I glance around. I hold up the shoe. "This is Porter's. He was here. He might be in there. Maybe Paige too."

Bezi runs her hands over the sides of her face. "I know. I just—"

"You're scared," I say. "Look at me. I'm scared out of my mind right now, but we gotta get Paige and Porter, and then we'll get as far away from here as we can. I don't care if we have to walk out."

Bezi nods. "If we're going in, let's not just walk through the front door."

We switch off our flashlights as we bypass the main entrance and move around the side of the building. I peer through the dingy windows, but the screens are so caked with dust and debris that it's hard to make out anything inside. At the rear of the building, there is another entrance, a doorway whose actual door has long since disappeared.

Stepping over the threshold, the scent of rot fills my nose. My eyes water and my throat feels tight. I hold still, hoping no one is here to notice our presence but also desperately praying that Porter is hiding somewhere inside.

A half dozen rooms occupy the first floor of the massive lodge. We sweep through a maze of empty sitting rooms and linen closets, almost all of them bare except for dead leaves and mice. The long center hall opens into an expansive foyer. A broken chandelier hangs from a rusted chain, and portraits of various pompous-looking men in strange black robes hang on the walls.

To the right of the double-spiral staircase that leads to the upper floors, there is a room whose intricately carved double doors sit slightly ajar. I push them the rest of the way open and find an office with a massive desk in the center. A taxidermic snow owl is perched on top of it. The room is ringed by built-in shelves, and they are all filled with moldering books.

I run my hand along the spines and read some of the titles aloud. "*Geological History of Upstate New York. Myths and Legends.*" I glance at Bezi, who is standing in front of a large, framed photo hung on the wall. "Who the hell was living out here?"

"The Owl Society," Bezi says.

"Who?"

Her gaze doesn't move from the photo, and I join her in front of it.

Bezi runs her fingers across a dusty silver plaque set into the bottom of the framed photograph. "It says The Owl Society, 1840."

The black-and-white photo shows a bunch of men standing on a large platform. As I lean in and shine my flashlight on the picture, I realize that it's set in the same location we'd just come from—the outdoor amphitheater in the grove. The photo is blurry, darker around the edges and lighter at the center. The men stand in three rows, but the faces of the ones in the back are unrecognizable. The owl carved into the oak looms over them, and a bright spot on the edge of the frame matches up to where the burning torch had been positioned.

"This has to be what Ms. Keane was talking about," I say. "She kept saying *them*. It's gotta be this Owl Society, right?"

Bezi nods as she circles the room. "It's a secret society?"

"Looks like it. But what are—were they doing?" It occurs to me in that moment that maybe this so-called Owl Society isn't some relic of the long-forgotten past. Somebody hurt Tasha, and Porter and Paige are missing.

On the wall next to the large photograph, there are smaller portraits in heavy brass and silver frames. Individuals in the same seated pose, all of them wearing black cloaks. The photos go from black-and-white to sepia to full color. Each portrait adorned with a small plaque.

Henry Woodsworth Hayward
Grand Owl, 1856

Johnathan Laurens Montevallo
Grand Owl, 1867

Lawrence Ulrich Davis
Grand Owl, 1872

More portraits ring the room, each of them featuring a man in the same pose, the same steely look in his eyes.

"What's a Grand Owl?" Bezi asks. "I don't like the way that sounds at all."

I'm not sure, but it looks like each of the men was a leader of this Owl Society at some point. The newest portrait is dated 1973.

"I wonder what happened after 1973," Bezi says. "They just disappeared?"

I think about Tasha and about what Ms. Keane said. Is it

possible they're still here? I suddenly feel the urge to bolt from the lodge and run as fast as I can back to the camp. I take Bezi's hands and prepare to do just that when something stops me.

A sound.

I hold my breath and angle my head toward the hall. "Do you hear that?"

Bezi stares at me wide-eyed, listening.

A muffled shriek sounds from somewhere nearby. I glance toward the window, still not daring to breathe. It sounds again and sends a bolt of unfiltered terror straight through me. It is the sound a person makes when they're in pain—when they're terrified. Tasha had made that noise when I approached her in the lodge, and someone else is making it now.

I glance down at my feet. The sound bleeds out of the cracks between the wooden floorboards, as if the house itself is screaming.

Bezi takes out her phone, glances at the screen, and shakes her head. Still no signal. We are alone and I have to make another snap decision. Everything in me is telling me to run away from this place as fast as I can and never look back, but the scream sounds again, and I swear there are words mixed in with the agonized cries. *Help me.*

I take a deep breath and try to put my thoughts together. "I need to find a way downstairs. Let's look for some stairs or a door or something."

Bezi nods, but I can see the hesitation in her pinched expression.

I lead her out into the hall and tiptoe through the corridor, looking for a way to the lower levels of the lodge. We move silently past a dated kitchen and I stop.

"What's wrong?" Bezi asks.

I duck inside the kitchen and approach the center island. It's strewn with bits of decayed leaves and broken sticks. Above me, the beams inside the ceiling are exposed, and the plaster that once covered them is scattered across the floor. I step through the pieces and pick up the thing that had caught my eye. It's a camera.

"Oh shit, Charity, is that Paige's camera?" Bezi asks.

I turn it over in my hands and press the "On" button. The little LED screen flickers to life, and I press the left arrow to scroll back through the photos. There are pictures of Bezi and Paige in the car. They're making faces and smiling wide. A knot crawls up my throat. I press the arrow over and over until I come to a series of photos taken in the dark without a flash.

There's a torch in the foreground, and a few hooded figures are gathered together. Trees crowd the frame. I press the button again, and the next photo shows the wooden platform in the grove. The hooded figures are standing atop it, and they have their hands raised in front of a man who is shirtless and bound at the wrists. I use the camera's zoom feature to look closely at the shirtless man's face. His eyes are wide, his mouth is slightly parted, and there is blood on his neck.

"Who is that?" Bezi asks as she peers down at the screen.

My mouth suddenly feels dry, and my hands begin to tremble. "I—I think it's Felix."

Bezi looks at me. "Felix?"

"He was supposed to run the office." My mind runs in circles. "He missed his shift. I thought he quit."

Bezi puts her hand on my shoulder, and I press the button to look at the next picture even though I'm scared to death of what I might see. The photo's a blur. The hooded figures are hazy, and Felix is lying on his back on the platform in the exact same spot where we'd found the bloody spot someone had tried to wash away. There's nothing after that. I turn the camera off and set it back down. I have to grip the edge of the counter to steady myself as a terrible thought claws its way to the front of my mind. "Heather and Jordan were no-shows too."

Bezi blinks once, twice, and then three times before she makes the connection.

"We need to keep moving," I say, pushing all those other thoughts aside. "Let's find Porter and Paige and get out of here."

Bezi nods, and we leave the kitchen, continuing down the hall. I find a narrow doorway near the rear of the lodge that is fitted with a series of dead bolts, but each of them is in the open position.

I exchange glances with Bezi, then put my palm against the door, grasping the handle with my other hand. I ease it open, hoping it doesn't protest too loudly. As I slowly pull it open, a faint orange light permeates the dark somewhere below. A narrow flight of stairs leads down into a hallway.

I take the steps one at a time, easing myself onto each one, then pausing as Bezi follows behind me. When we emerge into the hallway below, there is only one door at the very end, and it is sitting open.

A chorus of voices filters out, and the sound echoes down the hall. I can't make out what is being said but it sounds rhythmic, almost like a song. I grip my hands together to steady the trembling. From where I'm standing, I can just make out the subtle movement of shadows against the rear wall of the room at the end of the hall.

I duck down, pressing my back to the wall. "There are people in there," I whisper as Bezi ducks down beside me.

"What are they doing?" she whispers back.

I slowly stand and, keeping my back to the wall, make my way to the open door. Peering around the corner, I expect to find myself looking into another room, but instead there is a large rough-cut void, a cavernous opening that looks like it was carved out of the bedrock. It's sunken even lower than the hall we're standing in. A sloping ramp leads down to the floor of the cave-like room lit by a series of torches. There's a large structure in the center of the earthen floor. It looks like a wide wooden plank sticking straight out of the ground. Four figures in hooded black robes stand staring up at it, but from my position, I can't see what they're looking at. A strong odor of burned wood and something sweet, like incense, wafts into my face.

An unintelligible chant erupts from the room and Bezi jumps, knocking her knee against the open door. We duck back and try not to move or breathe. The chanting continues in a language I don't understand. And then someone begins to speak.

"Come forth," a gruff voice says.

One of the hooded figures steps forward and raises their arms toward the wooden structure. The chanting gets louder, becomes a frenzied loop of sounds. A hum permeates the air. The person's head drops, and I look at the ground in front of them. A dark substance is spilled across the earthen floor.

The deep, gruff voice speaks again. "Claim your power. Know that it will be yours. Accept no other outcome."

The hooded figure who had stepped forward begins to tremble under their robes.

"We have suffered terrible losses," the deep voice says. "But we will recover what once was ours. Through the blood. Through the ritual. Through the water."

I slowly lean forward to look into the cave again. The other three people in the robes have circled up in front of the wooden structure. They're entranced by whatever is on the side that's facing them, but I still can't see what it is. Suddenly, a figure steps into view, unfolding out of the shadows like a ghost materializing from the ether. I cup my hand over my mouth to keep from screaming.

An owl the size of a very tall person stands in the dancing firelight. Its mottled white and brown feathers are luminescent in the low light. Its eyes are like the ones in the carved effigy behind the crescent-shaped wooden platform in the grove—black and glinting. It moves to the center of the room.

"We have suffered losses, but our time has come once more," it says in the same gruff voice.

It takes me a moment to register that this is a man in a costume, but somehow, understanding that doesn't make it any better.

"We will reclaim our glory through blood, ritual, and the water," he continues. "Can you feel it?" He stretches out his bare arms and opens and closes his hands. "We are already on our way. We will return to the camp and use the ones who remain to solidify our position. We will feed the ravenous land. We will take what is rightfully ours."

The four onlookers bow low as they pull away their hoods and train their gazes on the strange wooden structure. There is suddenly a terrible ache in the pit of my stomach, an ominous feeling that takes my breath away—a crushing and all-consuming dread.

The people approach the structure and place their hands on it. With a groan, it rolls back, exposing the forward-facing side. There is something affixed to the front of it. Bezi gasps, and then the rush of blood in my ears blots out every other sound.

Porter's broken, bloody body is pinned to the wooden structure.

His eyes are open and blank, staring into nothingness. His gut is slit open, and everything that was inside is now on the outside. I begin to scream. I cannot stop myself.

CHAPTER 12

I am screaming so hard that I feel something rip inside my throat. The pain is hot and agonizing and it rockets through my neck as I stumble back. Bezi's hands are on me, shoving me away from the door. She puts her hand over my mouth, but it's too late. There's shouting and a rush of footsteps.

"Come on!" Bezi screams.

She pulls me along the hall and back up the stairs. We careen through the door and race down the hall. My body feels like it's moving in slow motion, like my limbs are too heavy. Behind me, the yelling sounds closer, the footsteps louder.

Bezi yanks the front doors open and we stumble down the steps, ducking onto the path that leads toward the grove. I glance back at the entrance to the lodge just as the person in the owl mask emerges like a monster stepping out of a nightmare. I see the human legs and bare torso, the long arms, but the owl's giant head is so realistic, it gives the impression that the person is half-human, half-bird. The person wearing it readjusts the headpiece as the four people I saw in the basement cave rush out of the lodge.

My legs are pumping and I have a death grip on Bezi's hand as we rush down the path. Bezi trips and falls.

"Oh hell no," I scream as I pull her up. "Not today! Get up!"

I don't care if I have to drag her away from this place; we are not stopping. I can almost hear Paige's voice in my head telling me how horror movies always have someone who trips and falls and that's when the killer closes in on them. If I want to live—if I want Bezi to live—I have to keep going.

Bezi pops up and keeps pace with me as I run faster than I have in my entire life. My lungs burn with every gasping breath. Even though adrenaline is rushing through my veins, I feel the pain in my muscles. I feel the air moving like wet cement through my lungs. I can't keep up this pace. When we've put some distance between us and the lodge, I stop and pull Bezi down into the brush just off the pathway. I clamp my hand over her mouth as she starts to protest, but not a minute later, a flurry of footsteps and flashlight beams descend on the path.

I hold my breath even as my heart beats wildly. Bezi shuts her eyes, clinging to me in the damp, dark underbrush.

"Where are they?" an angry voice shouts. From the darkened pathway, the figure in the owl headpiece emerges. "Where?"

"I lost them," a tall blond woman in billowing black robes says breathlessly.

"Well, find them!" barks the man in the owl mask. "We need them!"

"They probably retreated to the camp," another man says. "We need to stick to the original plan. Let's get there and do what we came to do."

The man in the owl mask paces directly in front of us. His pale feet crunch across the dirt not an arm's length from where we lay hidden.

"Our order will be renewed," the woman says. "We have shed plenty of blood already."

The man in the owl mask approaches her, and while the mask doesn't show his expression, his body does. His shoulders are pressed back, his fists are clenched, his breathing deep and steady.

"*I* say if it's enough," he says in a tone that confirms everything his body language has already revealed. He's not just angry; he's seething. "The Owl Society will regain its power and we will remake the world but only through the blood, the ritual, and the water. We will return to the camp and use the ones who remain." The owl mask's beady black eyes glint in the glow from their flashlights as the man leans so close to the woman, she has to lean back to keep them from making contact, but she does not step away from him. "I will make this land run red with the blood of a thousand camp counselors, children, adults—anyone. I don't care what it takes."

In unison, they bow to him, and then they all move off in the direction of the lodge. I don't move. I don't even breathe.

I worry that my heartbeat is loud enough for them to hear and that they'll come running back.

We wait. I don't know for how long, but we wait. Finally, when I'm positive they can't see or hear us, we make a break for the main road. We don't turn on our flashlights as we bolt past Ms. Keane's driveway as fast as we can. All I can think of is what the man in the owl mask said—"We will return to the camp and use the ones who remain." That has to mean Camp Mirror Lake, and the only people left are me and my friends. Images of Porter's eviscerated corpse flood my mind, and a wave of nausea sweeps over me. I grit my teeth and push it away as I hold open the gate at the rear of the camp so that Bezi can squeeze through. I follow her in, and we rush straight to the Western Lodge. I pull on the doors only to find them locked.

"Kyle! Open up!" I bang on the door, and there's a shuffling from inside. The curtain moves a little, and Kyle's dark eyes peer out at us. "Kyle! It's us! Open the door!"

The locks click open, and Kyle's face appears in the crack; he's holding a large kitchen knife in one trembling hand. I push my way through the door, and Bezi slams it shut. I slide the locks closed and lean against the door.

Kyle heaves a sigh and lowers his knife. "You scared the shit out of me."

I rush up to him and grab him by the arms as I struggle to catch my breath. "There are people in the woods! They're coming here to kill us! They killed Porter!"

Kyle's face is a mask of confusion. "What are you talking about?"

I peer around him and notice that Tasha isn't on the couch anymore.

"Where is she?" I ask.

"Javier called an ambulance and they came and got her, but Sheriff Lillard was with them," Kyle says. "And he didn't believe me when I told him what happened. He thinks everything is a damn prank or something."

"Did he see Tasha's wound?" Bezi shrieks. "How is that a prank?"

"He made it seem like we were messing around here, Charity." Kyle presses his lips into a tight line. "He said he was gonna come back up here and haul me off in handcuffs."

"Let him come back up here," I say. "He should be trying to figure out what happened to Tasha anyway." I picture myself punching Sheriff Lillard right in his face. I also picture me being sent to jail immediately for it. "You didn't go with them?" I ask, putting my hand on Kyle's arm. "I told you to go."

"I couldn't leave you." His bottom lip trembles as he looks down at the floor. "I knew you were still out there and—and—they killed Porter?" He sinks down onto the couch and holds his head in his hands. "I can't do this. What is happening?"

A white-hot anger ripples through me as I think of how smug and dismissive Sheriff Lillard was. I sit down on the couch next to Kyle and loop my arm under his. The weight of the situation threatens to crush me, but I hold myself together because there is something we have to do.

"We have to get to the office and make another call. We have to get help."

"Sheriff Lillard won't listen," Kyle says. "He might come back up here, but it's not gonna be till he's good and ready, and even then, he just wants to arrest us all."

"Fuck that guy!" Bezi shouts. "We call somebody else. We call somebody who *will* listen."

"Maybe Mr. Lamont?" Kyle offers.

That might not be a bad idea. He knows Sheriff Lillard is useless, and he doesn't seem like the kind of guy who plays around. He shut the game down immediately when he heard about what happened with Ms. Keane.

"Let's go," I say. "Right now. Those people said they were coming here tonight."

Kyle stands and shakes himself. "Okay. We go together?"

"Yeah," I say. "No more splitting up."

"Do you think Paige is still out there somewhere?" Bezi asks suddenly. Her eyes fill with tears, and she angrily bats them away. "We found her camera. She was there."

"You found her camera?" Kyle asks. "How do you know it was hers? And what does that mean? She dropped it or something?"

"It was hers," I say. "There were pictures of her and Bezi on it. And also pictures of . . ." The terrible images flash in my mind.

"Of what, Charity?" Kyle asks.

I shake my head. "Felix. And I think . . . I think these people, this Owl Society, killed him. Maybe Jordan and Heather too."

Kyle's lips part and his brow furrows. "How do you know that?"

"Because I saw what they did to Porter, and Felix is on that camera and Heather and Jordan are gone!" The words burst out of me like water from a dam. "They're all dead!"

A sob escapes Bezi's lips. "Tasha got away. I bet Paige did too. She's probably hiding out there like we were. And if those people are on their way here, that will give her enough time to get away and get some help."

I pull Bezi close to me as she sobs. "I'm sorry. I'm so sorry. I never should have said that. You're right. She could be out there." I have no idea if that's true or even a possibility, but it's what Bezi is leaning on, and I can't take that little bit of hope away from her.

• • •

Kyle grips the handle of his butcher knife and Bezi brandishes a broom. I unscrew the leg from the coffee table and hold it like a bat as we unlock the front doors and stand on the porch as the dark cloaks itself around us.

"Okay," I say quietly. "Let's move."

We walk toward the office single file—me in the front, Bezi in the middle, and Kyle at the back. Each of us scanning the surrounding paths, buildings, and clusters of pine trees. The exterior light from the boathouse illuminates the trail that leads from the Western Lodge to the office, but it's not enough to beat back the dark for more than a few feet. The waters of

Mirror Lake look like a black void, a gaping mouth just beyond the boathouse. The sentiment that was shared by the Owl Society and by Ms. Keane was that this land was hungry, ravenous, and I can hear the lake waters lapping against the shore like a monster wetting its lips.

I immediately pick up the pace, and as we reach the office, I find the door unlocked and slightly ajar. We crowd in and lock the door behind us.

Without turning on the lights, I tiptoe around the counter and grab the phone, dialing Mr. Lamont's number as fast as I can. I hit the wrong buttons and have to start over twice, but once I've got the right numbers punched in, I put the receiver to my ear.

There is only silence.

I slam it down and pick it back up. Still nothing.

Bezi switches on her flashlight and points it in my direction.

"Something's wrong," I say as a familiar dread washes over me again.

Kyle grabs the receiver and holds it to his ear. He slams the phone down and grabs the cord connected to the back. There's too much slack and when he pulls it, the frayed end appears in Bezi's flashlight beam.

"Somebody cut it," I say as I realize exactly what this means. I turn to Bezi and try to keep my voice steady enough to make her understand that we've made a terrible mistake. We don't have to wait for these people to show up. "They're already here," I say.

Bezi's eyes glint in the dark as her hands begin to tremble. Kyle stands as still as a statue, gripping his knife.

"What—what do we do?" he stammers.

I move to the window and peer out at the parking lot. Bezi's car is sitting in the cone of light emanating from the flood-light. It's too low to the ground, and I realize it's because the tires have been cut. I can hardly think straight. A wave of panic rushes over me, and I sit on the stool behind the counter.

I'm trying to survive. That's all I want—to get out of this place alive. I stare at Bezi and then Kyle, both of whom are silent and clearly scared to death. I am too. I shift my gaze to the office counter and see the game book sitting open, the names of the guests and staff penciled in.

I've been playing the part of a girl who escapes a serial killer every night for months. It's not a game this time. The consequences are real, but we still have to play.

· · ·

"I'm the final girl," I say. "It's literally my job to survive the night. We don't have any good choices here." I grab the game book and look at the roster, trying to think of a way to make any of this work in my favor. "It's just the three of us here for right now. Javier and Tasha aren't going to leave us here alone. I'm sure that as soon as they can, they'll get somebody else up here to help us."

"What about the pickup truck?" Kyle asks.

"We don't have the keys," I say. "Mr. Lamont has them, and even if he didn't, the tires are probably cut."

"Why would you say that?" Bezi asks, her eyes wide.

"Your tires are cut," I say.

A dreadful silence settles over us.

"We have to dig in and wait for help," I say. "Keep trying the cell phones. We'll get a spotty signal at some point, and we can use it to call Mr. Lamont, but until then, we have to play the game. We get our stuff together, we use the tunnels, we stay hidden. We survive the night. It's the only way we get out of here alive."

Kyle shakes his head. "I can't believe this is happening."

I put my hand on his shoulder. "They're not the only people who can put on masks and scare people."

We make our way back to the Western Lodge and bar the doors, cut out the main lights, and take stock of what we have to defend ourselves. It's not much, but it's all we have to work with—an assortment of dull kitchen knives, table legs, a half-empty can of bear spray, and the headsets we use to communicate during the game. We plug in our cell phones, and I help Bezi get her headset on.

"Just leave the channel open—that way you won't have to toggle it on and off," I say. "One of us should get to the control center and see if the cameras are still working. The lock on that outside door is the real deal, so you can lock yourself in there and be pretty safe."

"I'll go," Kyle says. "If the cameras are working, we can just avoid these weirdos until help gets here."

"Should we all go to the control center?" Bezi asks. "Just lock ourselves in there?"

"I know that's probably what we *should* do," I say. "But Paige might still be out there, and maybe if we can listen in on these people, we can find out if they know where she is."

"I thought we were gonna hide," Bezi says. "Now we gotta get close to them?"

"I'm not saying we go hunt them down. I'm just saying we need to keep our ears open in case they let something slip about Paige or Heather or Jordan."

Bezi nods, but fear is stretched across her face, pulling the corners of her mouth down. I close my hand over hers. Suddenly, there's a loud click, and the porch light on the lodge goes out. My phone buzzes, signaling to me that it's not charging anymore. The always-present electrical hum stops, and silence swallows the lodge whole.

"The power," Kyle whispers.

My heart ticks up. "The generator will keep the control center running for a few more hours. We gotta get over there."

Kyle sighs and pulls something out of his back pocket—the ghostlike mask he uses during the game.

"Put it on," I say.

He slips the mask over his head.

"That's terrifying," Bezi whispers.

"When you get to the control center, talk to me on the headset so we know you're safe," I say.

Kyle nods, takes a deep breath, and exits the lodge through the rear door. I lock it behind him, and then Bezi and I uncover the hatch in the kitchen floor. I slip my flashlight out of my pocket and shine it down the tunnel.

"Electricity's out down there too." I lean back and sigh. "If those lights are out, that means power to the main breaker is out. Everything in the entire camp is off that's not battery powered."

"Shit," Bezi says. "So what do we do?"

I cup my hand over my earpiece as I pick up the half-empty can of bear spray and slip it into my pocket. "Kyle? You okay?"

There's a rustling on the channel. The static is bad, but after a moment, Kyle's voice breaks through. "Yeah. I'm going . . . the pier. I thought . . . saw something by . . . lake."

"What? What did you see?"

"I don't know," he says, his voice tight. "Like . . . something white . . . feathers."

My hands are slick with sweat as I try to keep my voice level. "Keep going. Do not stop. Tell me when you get there."

There's a thud from somewhere above me. Bezi and I both freeze and tilt our heads up. We stare at the ceiling of the lodge as a slow march of heavy footsteps moves across it from somewhere outside.

"What is that?" Bezi asks.

I hold my breath.

Listening.

Something is on the roof.

CHAPTER 13

*T*hump. *Thump. Thump.*

The footsteps make their way up from the area over the eaves. We listen in horrified silence as I try to track the steps across the roof. My gaze traces along the wooden beams and stops . . . on the skylight.

The night sky outside the window is black, and the tops of the pine trees that surround the Western Lodge are visible only as even darker splotches against the inky sky. But as I stare up at it, something moves into the frame—a hazy white shape dotted with mottled brown splotches and two glinting black eyes.

Bezi sucks in a breath, and I quickly clamp my hand over her mouth.

"Don't move. He can't see inside," I whisper, recalling how

difficult it was to make out anything inside after I'd climbed up there to retrieve the dead bird.

The owl figure presses its very human hands against the glass. His torso expands and contracts like he's taking long, slow breaths. In and out, in and out. And then, after a moment, he disappears from the skylight, and his steps retreat down the opposite side of the roof.

"Did he see us?" Bezi asks, panic invading her voice.

"I—I don't think so," I stammer.

But we can't chance staying here. I yank Bezi toward the hatch in the kitchen floor, and we lower ourselves down just as the sound of glass shattering breaks the silence.

I pull the hatch closed above us and sprint down the tunnel. I fumble with my flashlight but can't get it to turn on while I'm running and dragging Bezi along behind me. I stumble over my own feet as we reach the end. From behind us, the hatch creaks open.

I climb up the ladder under the boathouse, and Bezi scrambles up after me as footsteps echo down the tunnel, rumbling toward us. Bezi moves to the door, but I stop.

"Wait," I say, panting.

"For what?" Bezi shrieks.

I grab an oar from the rack beside the stacked-up canoes and hold it high above my head. There's a scuffling at the bottom of the ladder, and then the blond woman I saw in the woods sticks her head out of the hatch. I bring the oar down as hard as I can, and it lands right on the top of her head with a sickening crack. She slumps forward, her torso on the ground in the boathouse, her legs hanging down the hatch. She groans and then lapses into unconsciousness as blood pools on the dusty floor under her head.

"Oh my god!" Bezi screams.

I lift the oar again, preparing to bring it down on the next person who pops up, but there's no one. It's quiet. I toss the oar aside and loop my arms under the woman's armpits.

"Help me, Bezi!"

Bezi grabs the woman's collar, and we wrench her up and out of the hatch. Bezi slams the trapdoor closed and slides a canoe over it as I tie the woman's hands and feet with a length of 550 cord we keep in the boathouse. She's breathing, but the blood is still flowing from her head in crimson rivulets.

I move to the door and peer out. The front doors of the Western Lodge are sitting open and the window overlooking the front porch is shattered. I cup my hand over my earpiece. "Kyle?"

The static crackles and pops, and then Kyle's voice comes out. "I'm here."

"Is the generator working? Can you see anything on the cameras?"

"Yeah," he says. "And somebody was in here when I showed up."

"What? Are you okay?"

"No," Kyle says, his voice trembling. "I—I had to hurt him. He jumped on me and—and . . ."

"Kyle, listen to me," I say. "It's not your fault. You did what you had to do."

He sighs into the mic. "I don't think he's dead, but I used my knife. Charity, am I gonna go to jail?"

My heart breaks open, and I'm so angry that he even has to think about that when all he did was defend himself against somebody who was probably trying to kill him. I worry that maybe Sheriff Lillard will say this is all our fault, that defending ourselves against these people is somehow worse than them trying to kill us.

"Don't worry about that right now," I say to him and to myself. "I need to know if you can see anything on the cameras."

There's a pause. "Some of the screens are out," he says, his voice choked with fear and worry. "Two people are turning over the staff cabins."

"There were four people in the room where Porter died." I swallow a knot in my throat and try in vain to push the image of Porter's mutilated body out of my head. "And then the guy in the owl mask. We took out the blonde."

"Took her out?" Kyle asks. "What does that mean?"

I glance back at the woman, who is still lying unconscious on the floor. "Doesn't matter."

"What now?" Kyle asks.

"We still don't know where Paige is," Bezi says.

I peer through the crack in the door and still see nothing. "I'm going to the staff cabins."

"*We're* going," Bezi says. "No splitting up, remember?"

I nod, and we gather ourselves. Stepping out onto the path in front of the boathouse, I tread lightly, trying to listen for footsteps, voices, anything to signal where the rest of these people are. All I hear is the steady ripple of wind across the surface of the lake and every few moments, some kind of disturbance of the water's surface. Maybe the grass carp jumping up to catch nighttime insects, maybe a bird swooping in to grab the fish, I don't really know, but every time I hear it, it fills me with a sense of terror.

I gesture for Bezi to follow me as we take the trail toward the staff cabins. We keep our lights off and try to move as quickly and quietly as possible. As we approach, beams from flashlights dart around inside my cabin and an echo of voices carries through the dark. I cut across the grass and duck down below the window, and Bezi sinks down with me.

"There's nothing here," a man grumbles from inside. "They already cleared out."

"So what do we do now?" another man says angrily.

I slowly stand and peer through the shade. A short man with gray hair is pulling out the drawers of my dresser and tossing them into a pile. A taller man with a shock of red hair and long, gangly arms and legs stands with his back to the window.

The gray-haired man massages his temple. "Alex, we cannot let this go. We need all of them if we're to be successful."

"You think I don't know what's at stake?" the redhead, Alex, says. "We are all that is left, and if we cannot salvage our Order, it will cease to exist."

"The Grand Owl would never allow that to happen," the gray-haired man says in a whisper. "To even suggest it is ridiculous."

Alex shakes his head. "He's powerful. I know that. I've seen what he can do, but can he bring us back from the brink? Maybe we're too far gone. What he's trying to do now feels impossible."

The gray-haired man sighs. "You've lost your faith in him?"

Alex shakes his head. "No. I trust him. But we need more blood, more sacrifices. We have held back too much. He wants to be conservative in his actions, and I just don't understand. We need drastic action."

"You know what happened last time we drew too much attention to this place," the short man says. "Some kid tried to re-create the ritual and failed miserably. The backlash almost ended our Order. It is the reason we find ourselves in the predicament we are in today. The Grand Owl will not allow something like that to happen again. He will keep this quiet, and he will not take any unnecessary chances."

"He'll have to find a way to get this land back under his control."

"A mistake we also have that kid to thank for," grumbles the gray-haired man. "Jesus. Our Order on the brink, the land and the power it holds that has always been ours, all lost because an outsider wanted what we had." He huffs. "I'd kill him if I could."

"It's been more than fifty years," says Alex. "He's an old man now."

"Still," the gray-haired man says. "I'd still like to do it."

They both nod, and I stare down at Bezi, who is listening with her hand pressed against her mouth. I crouch and press my mouth to her ear.

"They know who killed all those people back in '71."

Bezi nods her head, and I turn to peer back inside. My elbow knocks against the wood siding under the window.

"What was that?" the man called Alex asks.

I curse under my breath. A few seconds go by, and when I peer back through the window, Alex is staring me dead in the face.

My heart nearly stops, and I barely have time to grab Bezi and yank her up before both men are barreling out of the cabin.

"Run!" I scream as we cut through the towering pine trees and stumble onto the path that leads toward the showers.

Footfalls pound the ground behind me. Halfway down the path, a chorus of screams echoes through the camp. Despite the terror coursing through me, I stop. Bezi runs into me, nearly knocking me over. The men behind us also stop, raising their gaze to the surrounding woods.

"What the hell is that?" the gray-haired man asks.

Agonized screams ring through the camp. They echo in the dark, and it takes me a moment to realize Kyle must have cued up the sound effects. The hidden speakers cycle through screams and menacing footsteps. The sounds seem to be coming from every direction.

Bezi takes my hand and pulls me toward the showers,

and we're mounting the front steps before the men give chase again. We slam the door shut and wedge a trash can under the handle. With a loud bang, the men collide with the door. The can scrapes across the ground, and the gray-haired man slips his arm through the crack in the door and attempts to move it. I reach in my pocket and pull out the half-empty can of bear spray. I angle it toward the opening in the door and empty the canister directly into the faces of the two men. They immediately start to cough and gag, and I scramble back as a residual cloud of the noxious gas wafts into the shower building.

My throat burns and my eyes water uncontrollably. Bezi coughs so hard, she almost vomits. I run to the sink and turn on the water, flushing my eyes and mouth. There's a loud bang, and I spin around to see the angry faces of both men as they shove the door open a little more.

My mind runs in circles. The windows in the shower room are for venting only. They're high and narrow and impossible to climb through. There's no back door.

"What—what do we do?" Bezi stammers, a trail of spittle hanging from her chin, the whites of her eyes bloodshot.

I flush my eyes again, but my vision is blurry, my throat raw.

"Push harder!" screams the gray-haired man. "I'll kill her!"

My face feels like it's been exposed to an open flame, but in the wash of pain and fear, my nights of playing the final girl at Camp Mirror Lake give me a way out.

"The trapdoor," I say.

Bezi wipes her face with her shirt. "Huh?"

"Come on." I grab her and duck into the last stall.

There's no toilet there, just a rusted metal wall locker with a sign that says STORAGE hanging on the front.

"We're gonna hide?" Bezi asks. "They already know we're in here!"

I pull open the door and stare down into the darkened hole below. I push Bezi toward it, and she quickly shimmies down the ladder that leads to the second hidden tunnel. This one goes from the showers to the arts-and-crafts lodge on the south side of the camp. The tunnel is twice as long and unlit, but it's the only option we have.

The sound of wood splintering splits the air, and the two men fall into the shower building, tripping over themselves and shouting. The gray-haired man rushes me before I can get down the ladder and into the tunnel. He grabs me by the front of my shirt and slams me back against the wall. Pain rockets through my shoulder as the man's rancid breath blows into my nose and mouth. He smiles when he realizes he's got me pinned. He presses his forearm against my neck, and my vision starts to blur around the edges.

The man suddenly howls in absolute agony and lets up the pressure on my neck just long enough for me to bring my knee up in one quick motion, catching him right between the legs. He stumbles back and knocks into the man called Alex.

I duck into the wall locker and scramble down the ladder. As I make my descent, I catch a glimpse of the gray-haired man's ankle and understand why he was suddenly writhing in pain—a short carving knife is stuck in the tender flesh of his Achilles.

I jump the rest of the way down, and Bezi has her flashlight out, shining it into the tunnel.

"You stabbed him?" I ask.

She nods, her eyes wide, like she can't believe what she just did.

"I love you," I say.

Bezi grabs my hand. "Come on!"

We take off down the darkened tunnel. Behind me, someone comes crashing down, and then there's a loud bang and an anguished scream. I look back, and Bezi shines her light on the two men. Alex is crumpled at the bottom of the ladder, screaming like a wounded animal. Blood spurts from his shin, and the light from Bezi's flashlight glints off the shining white bone protruding from the torn skin. It's like he decided to skip the ladder, jumped, and landed wrong, snapping his bone clean in half. I can't look any more or I'll be sick, so I turn and run, pushing Bezi ahead of me until we get to the other end of the tunnel. Bezi climbs the ladder and pushes on the trapdoor above our heads.

"It won't open!" she screams.

I scramble up the ladder next to her and push on the hatch. It groans as we force it open.

A rush of footsteps sounds in the tunnel beneath me. I glance down to see the gray-haired man stumble to the bottom of the ladder. Bezi makes it up, and I climb up after her, my sweaty hands slipping on the rungs. I claw my way up, and just as I drag myself out of the opening, a hand clamps down on my ankle.

I'm pulled back into the mouth of the trapdoor. I kick and scream and try to dig my fingertips into the wood planks of the arts-and-crafts-lodge floor. The nails on my thumbs and forefingers break off, exposing the bloody pink beds beneath. I scream. I kick at the man behind me, driving my foot back as hard as I can. I connect with something soft. There's a groan, but the grip on my ankle doesn't relent. I'm pulled back again. My gaze darts wildly around the room.

"Bezi!" I scream. "Help me!"

Bezi is scrambling around in the dark, and the man is pulling me deeper into the hatch with each passing second. I search wildly for something, anything that I can use to defend myself with, when my gaze flits to a stack of archery quivers, each filled with arrows.

"Give me that!" I scream as I flail wildly in the direction of the arrows.

Bezi snatches one up and flings it to me. I grab a single arrow and allow the man to pull me a little closer so that I can roll over. When I'm close enough, I rear back and shove the arrow into the man's face as hard as I can.

He immediately lets go of me, and I clamber back as he howls in agony. I struggle to see in the dark, but as my eyes adjust, I make out the man's bloodied face and the arrow, its colorful fin drenched in blood, protruding from his right eye socket.

I jump up and kick the man squarely in the face. He tumbles into the darkness below, and when Bezi shines her light down on him, his uninjured eye is closed and his breaths come in ragged tears.

"Shut it!" Bezi yells.

I slam the hatch closed, and we push a heavy coffee table over it. I glance at Bezi, and her chest is heaving, her eyes wide. I quickly go to her and put my arms around her. She collapses against me and starts to cry. I want to cry, too, but I can't. My mind is numb with fear.

"Charity, what are we gonna do? We gotta get out of here. We need help."

I nod, but I don't know what to tell her. I rub her arms and press my forehead against hers.

"Charity?" a voice rings out.

I almost jump out of my skin. My earpiece is hanging against my chest, and I quickly stick it back in my ear.

"Kyle? Kyle!"

"Are you okay?" he asks. "I saw them follow you into the tunnel! Please tell me you're okay."

I'm not okay. Not even a little. "We gotta get out of here. Meet us at the office. We're gonna have to walk out or something. We can't stay here."

"Okay," Kyle says. "Meet you there."

Bezi and I leave the arts-and-crafts lodge and sprint back to the path that runs directly in front of Mirror Lake. The prerecorded screams are still echoing through the camp. It actually sounds louder than it was before. I touch my earpiece.

"Kyle? Can you cut the sound effects?"

Static echoes across the channel.

"Kyle?"

The sound effects cycling through screams and footsteps echo through the trees in every direction. Suddenly, Bezi grabs my arm and squeezes it.

I follow her gaze. At the head of the path, between us and the office, is a figure. Even draped in darkness, its outline is familiar, and it makes my blood run like ice in my veins. The beady black eyes of the owl mask glint in the illumination of the flashlight before I can switch it off. The owl man squares his shoulders. I can't see his face, but I know he's staring at me from under his shroud of mottled white and brown feathers.

CHAPTER 14

Fear cements my feet to the ground, and all I can hear are the automated screams and footsteps echoing in the darkness. And then he begins to speak.

"You have so much more fight in you than the others," the figure says. His voice is deep and resonant. It might have been soothing if it wasn't coming out of a man who has been hunting me and my friends like wild game.

"Where is she?" Anger bubbles up inside me. "Where is Paige?"

The man lifts his hand and points toward the lake. "Her blood soaks the ground and her body lies at the bottom of the lake, as does the boy's, as do the bodies of the ones before. Feed the land with blood and the lake with flesh, and anything you could ever want can be yours."

Bezi gasps as I gaze out over the rippling black water of Mirror Lake.

"You're lying!" I scream through a torrent of tears.

"Why should I lie?" he asks. "I'm telling you this because you must understand that your deaths will not be for nothing. Your sacrifice will usher in a new era for my Order. You should be honored."

"Honored?" I say through gritted teeth.

"Yes," says the man. He takes a step toward me, and he suddenly seems taller, more imposing than he did just a moment before. "Do you know how long this Order has been in existence? You were in our lodge. I know you saw what we did there, but you don't understand. How could you? Our rituals may seem barbaric, but they are the key to everything we once possessed."

"I don't care," I say angrily.

"Oh, but you should," he hisses from beneath the mask. "You were chosen, Charity."

A wave of confusion rolls over me. "How do you know my name?"

His shoulders rise just slightly. I don't know if he's smiling under that mask, but I feel like he is. "I know much more than that, thanks to someone very close to you. Someone who couldn't wait to see your guts splashed across these hallowed grounds."

My blood runs cold. Something had been digging at me. I felt it when I pulled that dead owl down from the roof and again when I saw those owl figures carved into the trees.

"You haven't put it together?" the man asks. "How did you come to be at this place, Charity? What was the thing that brought a lonely girl, whose own family couldn't care less if she lives or dies, here?"

I'd gotten this job because Mr. Lamont hired me, but it wasn't him who tipped me off about the job that first summer. It was someone else. Someone who couldn't wait to get me out of the house.

"Rob."

The man in the mask is smiling. I know it.

"Do you know what you can obtain by sacrificing your own family?" the man asks, as if I should have an answer. "It's a very special sort of thing."

Rob brought me the ad. Rob insisted I follow up on it. It was Rob who acted surprised every time I showed back up at home when the season was over. And it was in Rob's notebook that I found that sketch of an owl identical to the ones carved into the trees in the forest, and it was his taxidermic birds of prey, his owls, that watched me as I slept.

"He wanted me to die out here?" I ask in disbelief. "He—he knew about what you were doing?"

The man laughs. "A rumor led him to us. He thought he could curry favor by sending you here to die. Think of it as an act of goodwill, promises of what he was willing to do for us." A hissing sound erupts from under the mask, like he's blowing air out from between his teeth in disgust. "Unfortunately for him, he isn't the type of person I'd ever bring into the fold of our sacred Order." He laughs again, but it is an arrogant, boast-ful sort of sound. "We have used this power to chart paths for presidents, dictators, the wealthy, the elite. You have no idea the influence we once held." He tips his head back and sighs. "Your mother's pathetic excuse for a boyfriend was not worthy of benefiting from our rituals, Charity." He levels his head. "But I am."

The man crouches low to the ground, then springs forward and is suddenly standing directly in front of me. He towers over me, and the pale flesh of his chest heaves as a guttural growl erupts from his throat. He reaches for Bezi, and I instinc-tively grab his arm. He turns his attention to me, and his hand is around my neck before I can move. Bezi's screams fill my ears as the man lifts me straight off the ground and throws me across the path and into the side of the boathouse.

I strike the side of the building with such force that the air is violently expelled from my lungs in one painful exhalation. My vision goes black. I can't move or breathe or see anything for several moments. But I can hear, and Bezi's cries fill me with dread. The pain comes in a flood and tears through my body from my tailbone to my neck. I roll over and look up at the nighttime sky.

"Get away from me!" Bezi screams.

I roll up onto my elbow, and a fresh wave of agony crests over me. I swallow the vomit rising in the back of my throat and force my eyes to focus. The man in the owl mask is bearing down on Bezi as she scrambles away from him. He grabs her wrist and wrenches it sideways. There's a loud pop and Bezi yelps. I try to stand but can't get my legs to do what I want them to.

"Get away!" Bezi cries.

I grab hold of the boathouse and pull myself up. It hurts to move, but I lurch onto the path, grabbing a large stick from the underbrush. I stumble forward just as the man grabs Bezi by the sides of her head. The muscles in the backs of his arms flex as he presses in. Bezi isn't screaming anymore. She's clawing at his hands and at the mask, and little white feathers are swirling around in the air like snowflakes.

I raise the stick and bring it down across his back as hard as I can. The stick breaks in two, but the man doesn't flinch. I start to tear at the naked skin of his back when suddenly I hear a long, high whistle. I turn in the direction of the sound and see a tall, lumbering figure with their arm raised in front of them.

"Charity!" a familiar voice shouts. "Move!"

I duck out of the way, and a gunshot splits the air.

The man in the owl regalia lets go of Bezi, and she crumples to the ground. The man stumbles back and turns to face the figure. Blood pours from a hole in the center of the man's chest. The bullet has ripped straight through him. The white feathers are smeared with blood, and a gurgling sound is coming from under the mask. The man collapses to his knees, and I loop my arms under Bezi's and pull her away.

He wobbles and then falls face-first into the dirt. I stare at his body as it grows eerily still. A pool of blood fans out underneath him.

The other man ascends the steps to the office and looks back at me. "I'm calling the police," he says. He reaches into his pocket and steps inside the office. I scoop Bezi up and, supporting most of her weight on my aching body, I drag her to the office and up the front steps. Inside, I put her in the chair behind the front desk.

"Lock the door," I say to the man.

He does.

"Are you all right?" he asks.

"No," I say. I turn to him, and while I'm certain I know his voice, I can't place his face, though there is something familiar about him.

"Charity?" he says. "Why are you looking at me like that?"

I suddenly realize . . . it's Mr. Lamont. It's been so long since I've seen him face-to-face that I couldn't place him. I rush forward and wrap my arms around him, and he gently pats my back.

"Oh my god!" I sob. "That guy was trying to kill us! Him and some people in the woods! Mr. Lamont, we have to call the police."

"I did," he says. "They should be here soon. We just stay put till then." He sits in the extra chair by the window. "What kind of mess did I step into here, Charity?"

"I don't even know where to start," I say as I try to comfort Bezi, who I think is going into some kind of shock. I grab the first aid kit from under the desk and wrap her mangled wrist in an Ace bandage. "Porter and my friend Paige are dead." As the words leave my lips, they don't seem real. "I think Jordan and Heather too. And Felix . . . they're all dead."

"My god." Mr. Lamont sighs and shakes his head, a blank expression on his face. "And the others?"

"Javier and Tasha are at the hospital. Kyle is on his way here."

Mr. Lamont takes a tissue from his pocket and dabs at the sweat beading on his forehead. "Good. That's very good."

It finally feels like we've got someone on our side, someone who didn't hesitate to protect us when we needed it. I shudder to think of what would have happened if Mr. Lamont hadn't been there to stop the man in the owl mask. I go to the phone and pick up the receiver before setting it back down again. I momentarily forgot the assholes in the woods cut the line. I turn to Mr. Lamont, who's now standing. "Can I use your phone?"

"What?" he asks.

"Your phone? I should call . . ." I almost say I should call my mom, but I begin to think of what it means that Rob had a hand in sending me up here to die. Did she know what he was doing? I bite my tongue, trying desperately not to cry. "I should call Bezi's mom. I couldn't charge my phone after those people cut the power."

"Oh, I don't have a phone."

I glance at the landline and then back to Mr. Lamont, who

has moved to the window, where he's now peering through the curtain.

"You don't have a phone?" The words echo out of me, and time seems to slow to a crawl.

"No," Mr. Lamont says.

The room suddenly feels too small. "How did you call the police if you don't have a phone?"

Mr. Lamont turns and glances at the landline. He huffs out a laugh and reaches inside his coat. "Looks like I've put myself in a very awkward situation."

Bezi clutches my arm.

"What—what do you mean?" I ask. "And how did you know we needed help out here? We wanted to call you, but we didn't get a chance."

I take a single step toward the office door, and Mr. Lamont moves in front of it.

"Charity," Bezi says in a terrified whisper.

The corners of Mr. Lamont's mouth draw up in a sinister grin. Something in his expression shifts. Where before there was concern, now there is only malice, anger.

He clicks his tongue behind his teeth. "After all this time, a final girl finally caught up with me." He shakes his head. "Predictable."

"Mr. Lamont?" I don't even recognize my own voice now.

"Don't be afraid, Charity," Mr. Lamont says. "This will all be over soon."

CHAPTER 15

Mr. Lamont produces a revolver from his coat and points it directly at my chest. Whatever hope I was clinging to of a rescue, of getting someone to help us, bleeds out of me.

"Let's take a little walk," he says, unlocking the door with one hand while keeping the gun trained on me and Bezi with the other. He gestures for us to go outside. I hesitate.

"They might still be out there," I say. "Please, Mr. Lamont."

He motions again. "We don't need to worry about them. Move."

Bezi puts her uninjured hand on my back as I walk out the door and down the steps. Mr. Lamont follows close behind. As we walk past the lifeless body of the man in the owl mask, Mr. Lamont grunts. I stop and turn to him as he crouches and removes the mask from the dead man's body. I don't know what I expected to see under the mask, but it's definitely not a balding middle-aged man. The way he flung me around like I was nothing, the way he scaled the roof—it doesn't make sense.

"You have questions," Mr. Lamont says as he tucks the owl mask under his arm. "And I have answers, but we need to move into the Western Lodge first."

Mr. Lamont prods us forward, and we move toward the main lodge. From over my shoulder, there's a splash in the lake, like something heavy has been dropped into it. I glance back.

"Keep moving," Mr. Lamont says.

There's suddenly a flurry of footsteps, and Kyle comes racing down the trail.

"I was looking for you!" Kyle says. "I—" He registers Mr. Lamont and then the gun.

"It's a party," Mr. Lamont says in a flat, emotionless way.

Kyle lets his arms fall to his sides as his mouth forms a little O.

"Fall in line," Mr. Lamont orders.

Kyle raises his hands in front of him. "Please. Please don't hurt me."

Mr. Lamont flicks the gun, gesturing for Kyle to move. He stumbles over to me and stays behind me as we all go into the lodge single file. Mr. Lamont gestures to the couch, and I help Bezi take a seat while Kyle settles next to her. I go to sit down when the tip of my sneaker bumps up against something partially hidden under the couch. It's dark. I'm having trouble seeing, but as my eyes adjust, I realize it's a hand, clenched into a bloody fist, and on the wrist is a bright pink hair tie. I stumble back and fall hard onto the ground. From the floor, I have a clear view of Tasha's and Javier's bloodied faces. Their bodies lie tangled together under the couch.

A scream claws its way up my throat and erupts from behind my lips. My cries split the air, and Mr. Lamont delivers a swift kick to my leg.

"Get up," he growls.

I pull myself onto the couch, and I can feel the soft bulges of Tasha's and Javier's corpses through the thin fabric. Bezi leans against me, sobbing. The orange glow from the fireplace washes the room in a gauzy light, and Mr. Lamont stands backlit by the flames, like a monster emerging from the depths of hell.

"You killed them," I say through a blur of tears. "You're with those people from the woods."

Mr. Lamont narrows his eyes at me. "No. Not with them." He keeps the gun trained on me as he speaks. "Do you know where you are right now?"

I exchange glances with Kyle. "I don't know what you mean," I say.

"Of course you don't," Mr. Lamont says dismissively. "This particular piece of land has been used for generations by those Owl Society folks."

Mr. Lamont points the gun at me and clenches his jaw, then smiles.

"That's what they call themselves," Mr. Lamont says.

"They've always been here. They stole this land from the folks who were here before. Been conducting their meetings and rituals in the forest around here ever since. Seeding the land with blood and giving the flesh over to the lake."

My mind goes in circles. "The man in the owl mask told me."

Mr. Lamont tilts his head. "Did he now?" He seems irritated. "He was a regular chatty Cathy with you, huh? I couldn't get him to tell me a damn thing. Did he tell you about the ritual too?" He drags his hand across his gut in the same spot where Porter was sliced open. "Spill the blood on the ground, dump the corpse in the lake, recite the words. Not necessarily in that order." He shakes his head and toes at the floor with the tip of his boot. "They could have anything they want, but the price—the price always has to be paid in blood and in flesh."

"Did you know my mom's boyfriend sent me up here to die?" I asked angrily.

"Of course," he says like it should be obvious. "Sent you up here to be sacrificed. But they wouldn't let it happen." He huffs. "Who does he think he is? He hasn't done the work or put in the time. He hasn't given everything he has to—" He stops short, pursing his lips and grunting angrily. "Doesn't matter now."

"But you're not with them? You're not with the Owl Society?" I ask, setting aside the seething hatred I have for Rob to deal with what's in front of me right at this moment. "Why are you holding us at gunpoint?"

Mr. Lamont looks to each of us as if he's weighing how

much he wants to say. He finally sighs and continues but keeps the gun pointed at me. "The Owl Society has run their dubious little social club from the Mirror Lake area for generations. But by the sixties, they got greedy. Stopped letting new folks into the society so they could hold on to the power for themselves. Then one of their leaders up and died, and everybody who was left took what they wanted and left. A few of them sold off the land to turn a quick profit. My father stepped in and bought it but, being the visionary he was, he saw an opportunity." Mr. Lamont shifts the gun from one hand to the other. "My father and the remaining members of the Owl Society made a deal. My daddy would start a camp, bring up vulnerable kids, kids nobody cared about. Kind of like you, Charity."

I'm so taken aback by his abrupt departure from the story that I gasp.

"Your mama doesn't take good care of you, does she?" Mr. Lamont asks. "Don't really call to check up on you. I think that's what Rob saw in you—a girl whose own mama doesn't even care about her. Hell, you could turn up missing and maybe she wouldn't even notice, isn't that right, Final Girl? Is that why you didn't think about calling her first? Because you know she won't care?"

I stare into the fire, and the tears spill down my cheeks. I hate everything he's saying because it's true.

"So my daddy sets up shop," Mr. Lamont continues like he's telling a bedtime story and not like he's spilling the most heinous details of this entire operation. "He builds the camp and lets the Owl Society pick off campers at will. Each body in the lake is a little bit like a toll you pay to get access to something you want, except this isn't a fairy tale. There's no three-wish limit. The only thing keeping them in check was how secretive they were. Too many missing folks would be too obvious." Mr. Lamont smiles coldly. "They kept the money coming and my father never asked questions. He was happy with cold hard cash, but he should have demanded that they share their secrets with him. He could have done so much more. He could have *been* so much more." His eyes are like voids as he continues rambling. "I went to their lodge out there in those woods. I watched them kill campers, hikers, anyone really. But their incantations weren't anything I recognized. I couldn't decipher them fully, so I did what I could and when the opportunity presented itself, I spilled enough blood to appease whatever ancient power demanded it, and what did I get? Nothing."

I scoot forward on the couch as Javier's call with his grandmother echoes in my head, along with the words of Alex and the gray-haired man. Everything suddenly clicks into place. "The killings at the camp in 1971."

Mr. Lamont's head snaps up, and he slaps his knee, smiling. "You're so good at your role, Charity. Final girls always figure it out, don't they?" He laughs. Actually laughs, and I want to throw up. "I was seventeen. I'd known about the Owl Society my whole life and I thought—well—I thought I could show them that I deserved to be among them. I cut down six people at the camp that summer. Six. Spilled their blood on the earth, fed their corpses to the lake, and said the words I could remember out loud."

Kyle sniffs, and only then do I realize he's crying a river of silent tears.

Mr. Lamont looks down at the ground. "It couldn't give me what I wanted, or maybe I didn't do it right."

"What did you want?" Kyle asks.

Mr. Lamont looks up at him. "My mama died when I was six. I think my daddy put her in that damn lake thinking he'd get something he wanted. All *I* wanted was to have her back."

Silence engulfs us for a long time before Mr. Lamont speaks again.

"It all went to shit after that," Mr. Lamont says. "The camp closed. The Owl Society members went underground, and I had to wait for my own father to die so that I could take over here. I never really got what I wanted, and neither did he." His voice sounds far away now, like he's remembering something. "Imagine my delight when those Hollywood folks came around asking if they could make a movie here. They didn't even know what happened in '71. They were just scouting for a location, and there I was. I let them shoot their little movie here on the grounds, on the condition that I could give some input. They loved my ideas—a masked killer who grows stronger with every kill!" He slaps his leg and grins. "You saw that freak with the mask. He probably asked for that power, that strength. And there I was, a kid hoping to bring his dead mama back from the grave." His gaze becomes steely again. "We all want something different."

There's a knock. Mr. Lamont smiles and backs up toward the door. He flips the lock and in walks Ms. Keane, a bandage wrapped around her head and carrying a machete a foot long. I jump up, and Mr. Lamont points the gun at me.

"Sit," he barks.

I don't. I stay standing as Ms. Keane nuzzles up to Mr. Lamont. He kisses her on the top of her head, and she locks the door.

"What is this?" Bezi asks.

"What does it look like?" Mr. Lamont asks. "My wife wants in on the fun. It's only right."

"I can't believe you," Kyle mumbles under his breath.

Ms. Keane marches up to him and smacks him so hard, a mist of spittle sprays from Kyle's lips.

"Shut up!" she screams in his face, gripping the handle of her weapon so hard that her knuckles pale. "You've been betraying us this whole time, you selfish little bastard! You dug up that bird and put it on the porch, hoping they'd get scared and leave." She balls her hand into a fist. "You had to hide the keys and cut the tires and I could barely get you to do it without you crying like a baby. You're so goddamn worthless!"

I turn to Kyle and watch as sweat cascades from his forehead, dampening the collar of his shirt. He cowers in front of Ms. Keane.

"You think I don't know that you were hiding out there when these two and that other little brat showed up to our house?" she says angrily. "I knew you were out there! Sneaking around! Betraying your family! You're pathetic!"

Kyle doesn't look at me.

I recall how he disappeared as Ms. Keane held us at gunpoint but he also saved us.

"You—you told me Tasha and Javi left in an ambulance," I stammer as all the terrible pieces start to fit together.

Ms. Keane looks back and forth between us, and a smirk spreads across her wrinkled face. "Oh, how fun. We haven't gotten to the part where you find out that he's *our* grandson."

"Kyle . . ." I can't even think of what to say. The betrayal is crushing.

He stands and moves behind his grandparents like the coward he is, and I look away from him.

"Time to get moving," Ms. Keane says. She reaches into her pocket and pulls out a bundle of zip ties, tossing them to Kyle. "Tie them up."

Kyle doesn't hesitate. He takes the zip ties and restrains Bezi first and then comes to stand in front of me. He loops a zip tie around my wrists and pulls it tight.

"I thought we were friends," I say. "I thought you were helping us."

He looks down at the floor. "I—I was."

Ms. Keane shoves him out of the way and pushes me and Bezi toward the front door. "Shut up."

As she prods us forward, the tip of her weapon grazes my back. There's no chance I can get away from her without her slashing me. As we emerge from the lodge, there's a loud creak as the door to the boathouse yawns open. The blond woman Bezi and I tied up is stumbling out of the little wooden structure, her hair matted and crusty with blood.

She registers Mr. Lamont, and her eyes widen. "Y-you bastard!" she hisses.

Mr. Lamont raises his gun and fires a single shot. The snap echoes through the dark, and the woman collapses in a heap.

Bezi screams, and Ms. Keane shoves her so hard that she falls forward into the dirt. I shoulder-check Ms. Keane, and she stumbles back before charging at me with her machete raised in front of her. I throw my hands up, but Kyle steps between us.

"Grandma!" he shouts. "Just stop!"

"Don't tell me what to do," she snaps. "Not when you've been sneaking around helping these people out. They could have gotten away. We need them, and you risked all of that because of your bleeding heart." She spits on the ground at his feet.

A gurgling sound comes from the blond woman, but after a moment it stops, and she lies too still to be alive anymore.

Mr. Lamont tucks the gun into the waist of his pants and awkwardly shoves the dead woman back into the boathouse and shuts the door. Ms. Keane pushes me and Bezi toward the lake. When we reach the rocky shore, Ms. Keane kicks me in the back of my knee, and my legs fold under me. She does the same thing to Bezi, and soon we're leaning on each other, hands bound, as Mirror Lake's black waters lap against the dock.

Ms. Keane turns to Kyle and narrows her eyes at him. "Go get them."

Kyle skulks off toward the lodge as Mr. Lamont rejoins us and stares out over the water.

"The one in the tunnel," he says, glancing over his shoulder at Ms. Keane. "Did you handle it?"

She nods enthusiastically. "And the one with the arrow in his eye." She claps her hand down on my shoulder. "That was a real good thing you did, sweetie."

I shrug away from her. "So you've been watching us?" I ask, trying to work my wrists around, but the zip tie cuts into my skin with every movement.

"Of course," Mr. Lamont says. "The cameras came in handy. I did see that you found my little stash in the control center." He chuckles. "You can't fault me for wanting to keep a few mementos. It's funny how no one ever connects the dots. A camper goes missing, a hiker goes off the grid, even kids—people care about the kids least of all. And all the while, it was them—the glorious order of the owl—the Owl Society."

"We'll do better than they ever did," Ms. Keane says.

"What?" Bezi asks.

Mr. Lamont looks like he's about to answer when Kyle returns. He's got Tasha's lifeless body draped over his shoulder. Bezi turns her face away, and I bite my tongue so hard that it starts to bleed.

Kyle sets her down on the ground, then leaves, returning a few moments later with Javier's corpse. He lays him next to Tasha, then stands off to the side, his eyes downcast.

"Do it," Mr. Lamont says. "Feed the lake." He begins to chant something in a language I can't recognize. The words flow out of him like he's rehearsed it a million times. Ms. Keane and Kyle grab ahold of Tasha and carry her to the end of the pier, where they toss her body into the murky depths. They walk back and do the same thing to Javier. Mr. Lamont stumbles over the last recitation of the words, then stops and tilts his head back.

"You messed it up," Ms. Keane says angrily.

"Only that last part," Mr. Lamont says. "It still should have worked."

"You're saying it right?" Kyle asks.

Mr. Lamont shoots him a dagger of a glance. "I know what I'm doing! Maybe if they'd have just invited me to be one of them, I wouldn't have to get my information secondhand." He turns to Ms. Keane. "I think the words have to be spoken while the sacrifice is being performed, not after." He leans close to her. "We have these two. The ground is soaked in blood. The lake has been filled with bodies. We can sacrifice these two and be more powerful than any of the Owl Society members could have ever dreamed. We don't need to remake the world the way they wanted. It can just be me and you and whatever we want."

"What about me?" Kyle asks.

Mr. Lamont and Ms. Keane look at him like they've just remembered that he's even there.

"You didn't say anything about me," Kyle says.

"You'll get what's coming to you," Mr. Lamont says. "We have to be careful. Let me and your grandmother do this first; then we'll talk about you."

Kyle presses his lips together. "The ritual can give you anything you want?"

Mr. Lamont stares at him.

"I'd use it to get as far away from the two of you as I could," Kyle says.

Ms. Keane huffs. "Stupid boy."

"You're not stupid," I say, seeing an opportunity to appeal to whatever might be left of Kyle's humanity. "These people don't give a shit about you, and you don't have to do what they want."

Ms. Keane approaches me in a rush and hits me in the back of my head with the butt of the machete. Everything goes black for a moment, and then I'm lying on the rocky shore, watching as Ms. Keane and Kyle hold Bezi down. Mr. Lamont slips the owl mask over his head and bellows the incantation aloud. My vision blurs as I try to turn over, but I feel like I can't move. My body won't do what I want it to.

Ms. Keane hands Mr. Lamont something shiny—her machete.

Bezi screams.

Blood colors the rocks beneath her as I cry out in the dark.

I reach for her, but she doesn't reach back. She lies on her back, her eyes wide and empty.

Mr. Lamont rears up, a shudder running through his body. He touches his exposed arms, opens and closes his hands.

"I did it," he whispers. "I did it! Put her body in the lake! Now!"

Suddenly, there are two quick pops, and Mr. Lamont staggers back, clutching his chest where a bloodstain blooms on his dingy white shirt. He falls back. His head and upper torso bob in the water at the lake's edge.

"No!" Ms. Keane screams as she rushes to Mr. Lamont's side. "No! Kyle! What did you do?" She cradles her husband's head, still covered by the owl mask.

Kyle approaches her, and there are two more pops. Ms. Keane's body splashes into the lake next to her husband.

I struggle to pull myself up to sitting, and I'm afraid to reach my bound hands up to touch my head because it feels like a piece of my skull might be missing. I shut my eyes as Kyle's footsteps move around behind me and splash into the lake water. I don't want to open my eyes. I don't want to see Bezi's body on the shore. I can't.

I groan and Kyle is suddenly there, pulling me up to standing. I still don't want to open my eyes. I lean against him.

"Oh, Kyle," I say through my tears. "Bezi. We gotta get help."

I have my cheek pressed against his chest as he mumbles something against my hair, but I can't quite make it out. When I pull back, keeping my eyes down to avoid seeing Bezi, something cold, something wet sticks to the skin at the side of my face. I lift my still-bound hands and paw at my cheek. When I pull my hands away, a scattering of white feathers sticks to my fingertips.

I look up. Kyle's face is cloaked by the soaking wet owl mask. He utters the incantation and, in one quick motion, draws Ms. Keane's machete across my abdomen.

The pain is white hot for a brief moment, and then there's nothing. No feeling as my insides spill out across the rocks. Kyle slips his arms around me and lifts me up.

I see the stars. My heart sputters in my chest.

Footsteps. Wooden beams creaking. My vision blinks on and off. On and off.

There is a splash, and my body is wrapped in a blanket of cold. I gasp, and the cold spills down my throat. I see Kyle standing at the end of the pier as I slip below the surface. The feathered owl mask looks ghostly through the rippling water. The cold is gone now. The pain too. It's just me and the inky waters of Mirror Lake.

EPILOGUE
ONE YEAR LATER

Bezi

I sit on a bench on the south shore of Mirror Lake, looking out over the black water. The forest is starting to reclaim most of the buildings that weren't razed. Remnants of the Western Lodge's foundation poke up out of the foliage, giving a little clue to what was there before.

I hope that one day, the forest will take back everything from this cursed place.

I breathe in the chilly nighttime air. I know I shouldn't be here. Technically, it's off-limits to everyone except law enforcement because they are still pulling body parts from the lake even after all this time. But not Charity. She's still down there, and that means I am too. I'm here because somebody has to bear witness. Somebody has to remember.

I touch the jagged scar that runs across my abdomen. Six

surgeries later and things still aren't the same, but the scars remind me that what happened to me and to Charity and everyone else was real. Sometimes it seems so much like a nightmare that I wonder if one day, I'll wake up and find that it was all just an awful dream. Now I'm the final girl. A title I took from Charity—one I wish almost every day I could give back to her.

I should have died right here on the shore of Mirror Lake, but I didn't. And as it turns out, my frantic call went through, but the 911 operator thought my pleas for help were some kind of sick prank. It took them hours to actually reach me, and by the time they showed up, Kyle was long gone.

Unlike before, when people had died at Mirror Lake and the whole thing had been hushed up, the media turned its full attention to me in the aftermath of what people were calling a real-life sequel to *The Curse of Camp Mirror Lake*. I was the final girl, and there wasn't any way to get away from the photographers and the journalists looking for a good spin on the tragedy that had unfolded here. They wanted me to talk about what it had been like to play dead for hours or what it had been like to realize the things unfolding at Camp Mirror Lake were so much worse than the events Charity and the staff had re-created as part of the terror simulation.

That's how it went for months. It wasn't until the following summer that things seemed to calm down. The press was on to the next, more interesting thing, and all I was left with was the grief and the sadness and the scars.

Paige, in her obsession with slasher films, had always talked to me about the rules. She was the one who seemed to know how that night, exactly one year ago, would go. It was her voice that drove Charity and me to make the decisions we did. It's her voice I hear now as I sit at the edge of Mirror Lake in the dark.

"The final act is never really the end," she said to me and Charity once as we watched the original *Friday the 13th* under a pile of blankets on a chilly Halloween night when we were about thirteen. "There's always a twist, but it only works if you don't see it coming."

I watched the whole movie through my fingers, and when Jason Voorhees's mother had her head removed by that movie's final girl, I breathed a sigh of relief. Paige smiled at me and told me to keep my eyes on the screen. I almost choked on a piece of pizza when Jason's decomposing corpse reappeared from the depths of Crystal Lake.

As I sit here now, I think of Paige's words again. She was always right.

I stick my hand in my coat pocket and pull out the folded letter that arrived in my mailbox three weeks ago. It came on a Saturday morning, and there was no postmark or return address on the letter at all. That told me that whoever delivered it had brought it to my house and put it in the mailbox themselves.

When I first read it, I thought it was a joke. An awful prank that somebody who had seen all the press about the murders at Camp Mirror Lake was playing on me. But as I read and reread the letter, my gut feeling was that it was real, and that was more terrifying than anything.

I take out the letter as I sit very near the spot where Charity died—where a part of me also died. A part that, as hard as I tried, I could not bring back to life. I unfold the letter and read it for the thousandth time.

I'm sorry, Bezi. I don't know if you believe me or if you even care, but I have to say it. I should never have helped them. I didn't have a choice. I got what I wanted. I'm free from them, but I think about what I had to do to have this. I'm sorry. But I have something I can share with you. I think you know what it is. Maybe it can make up for what I did. You can have money, strength, power, whatever you want.

If you want, meet me at the place where it happened on the day it happened. If you're not there, I'll assume you never will be.

It was from Kyle.

There is no one else it could have come from, and he put it in my mailbox with his own two hands. I didn't take it to the police. I didn't tell anyone he'd sent it. I simply put an X on my calendar and waited.

The fear of him that lived in my mind and guided my entire life since that terrible night evaporated as soon as I accepted that he had written the letter. He knows where I live. If he wanted me dead, I'd be dead. But it seemed like he was trying to make amends somehow.

And now it's time. One year to the day after the massacre at Camp Mirror Lake.

The place where it happened. The day it happened.

I shove the letter in my pocket and wait.

A branch breaks in the woods, and I angle my head to the right. Footsteps move closer as the soft sounds of the forest fade away. Almost as if the creatures that live there know they're in the presence of a monster. From the tree line, a figure emerges, draped in shadow.

"Bezi," a voice calls.

I recognize it.

I recognize him.

He steps out of the dark and into the dappled light of a nearly full moon, and I have to ball my fists in the pockets of my jacket and clench my teeth together to keep from running up on him. I want to tear him apart with my bare hands.

"I didn't think you'd come," Kyle says. He edges in with his back to the lake, keeping a wide distance between us.

"I almost didn't," I lie. There is nothing that would have stopped me from being here.

"I'm glad you did," he says.

He looks taller and a little more gaunt than the last time I saw him, which was when he stepped over me, thinking I was dead, and disappeared into the dark like some kind of ghost.

"You said you were going to share something with me," I say, trying to keep my voice steady.

He nods and takes a step toward me. "This." He takes from

his pocket a piece of folded paper and holds it out in front of him. "It's the incantation that the Owl Society used. That my grandfather used when he—"

"When he thought he'd killed me," I say.

Kyle nods. "He thought he'd succeeded. But you didn't die and your body didn't go in the lake, so it wouldn't have worked anyway."

I take the paper from him, but I don't unfold it. I don't need to.

"What is it you think this will help me with?" I ask as I stare into his eyes without blinking.

He shrugs and kicks at the rocks on Mirror Lake's shore with the toe of his shoe. "I don't know. Whatever you want."

I press him. I want to know how he thinks this will make amends. "What does that mean?"

He comes another step closer. "You can have anything you want. Or almost anything. My grandfather didn't get what he wanted the first time around when he killed all those kids."

A shudder runs through me. "What did he want this time around?"

"Money, fame," Kyle says, shaking his head. "Maybe that's not so bad."

"And you think that's what I want?" I ask, looking up into his face that is now covered with a length of unkempt beard. "You think power, or money, or influence will make this better?"

He shakes his head. "I'm not saying it can undo what happened, but think about it—what if you never had to worry about money or what if you wanted to be in charge? Come on, Bezi. The Owl Society has been using this power for whatever they want. Why shouldn't you use it to get something you want?"

"It requires a sacrifice," I say.

Kyle gestures to the lake. "Do you know how many bodies are in there? How many people have been sacrificed to the land and the lake? What's one more if it means you can have some peace?"

I glance down at the ground, then back up to Kyle. "You know what, Kyle? You're absolutely right."

He smiles and nods, clapping his hand down on my shoulder.

I quietly slip the knife from my pocket and stick it into Kyle's abdomen, just below his ribs on the right side. I grasp the handle with both hands and drag it across his belly. There is a terrible ripping sound, a warm splash across my hands.

I chant the Owl Society's incantation aloud.

I don't need the paper Kyle gave me. I remember every syllable from the night he spoke the incantation as he murdered Charity and as Mr. Lamont tried to do the same thing to me. The words are burned in my mind.

Kyle's eyes grow wide. A gurgle erupts from his throat as he staggers back, clutching at his stomach. My heart pumps furiously as I scream the incantation at him. His blood spills across the ground, and his feet splash into the murky lake water. He collapses to his knees and sways from side to side.

I approach him slowly, still gripping the knife, a white-hot rage coursing through me like electricity. I finish the last of the secret words and plant my foot directly in the center of Kyle's chest. I shove him back as hard as I can, and he falls into the water. The light fades from his eyes as his corpse bobs in the shallows.

I retake my seat on the bench and close my eyes. I concentrate on the thing I want most. I wonder what the other people who had access to this knowledge concentrated on when it was their time to collect the rewards their sacrifices won them.

For me, there's no amount of money or power or influence that will suffice to ease the ache I feel in my chest. Only one thing can do that—one person.

"Me and you till the end of the world, right?" I whisper into the dark.

There is a splash somewhere in the lake.

I keep my eyes closed.

Another splash and then the sound of water spilling onto the crumbling pier, as if shed from the body of a swimmer exiting a pool.

The creak of aging wood planks under someone's weight.

The shuffle of footsteps.

I keep my eyes closed.

The footsteps come closer, stepping off the wooden pier and shuffling across the rocks until they're right in front of me.

I lift my chin and open my eyes.

"Charity."

ACKNOWLEDGMENTS

I love scary stories. I always have. I'm an '80s baby and came up in a time when slasher movies were enjoying a huge revival. Jump-started by John Carpenter's 1978 film, *Halloween*, the early '80s saw over a hundred similar films that mirrored the *Halloween* template—killer stalks teens through increasingly violent scenes, usually resulting in one person surviving it all . . . the Final Girl.

You're Not Supposed to Die Tonight is my ode to slasher flicks and the Final Girls who survive them only to inevitably have to run from their assailants in countless sequels and spinoffs. From *Halloween*'s Laurie Strode to *A Nightmare on Elm Street*'s Nancy Thompson and *I Know What You Did Last Summer*'s Julie James—Final Girls deserve their time in the spotlight. It is my love of horror movies that drove me to write this story and I had so much fun crafting this tale. Fun fact, I share a birthday with scream-queen Neve Campbell from the iconic Scream franchise. Sidney Prescott fans, stand up!

I'd like to extend my sincere thanks to my agent, Jamie. Going from fantasy to horror was a big leap but I couldn't have done it without your support. To my editor, Mary Kate Castellani, thank you for helping get this story in shape. Everything about this book is better because of your insight. Huge thank-you to the entire team at Bloomsbury. Special thanks to cover artist Fernanda Suarez, who also did the cover art for the UK edition of *Cinderella Is Dead*. Your work is stunning!

Huge thank-you to Mike, Amya, Ny, Elijah, Lyla, and Spencer. Love you all so much!

And to my readers—thank you for all your support! I hope you enjoy this story. I hope it makes you reconsider turning out the lights before you go to bed. Happy reading, my friends.